I0583647

# HUNGRY FOR

# LOVE

*Rick R. Reed*

A NineStar Press Publication

Published by NineStar Press
P.O. Box 91792,
Albuquerque, New Mexico, 87199 USA.
www.ninestarpress.com

# Hungry for Love

Printed in the USA
First Edition
May, 2020

Print ISBN: 978-1-64890-001-3

Also available in eBook, ISBN: 978-1-951880-98-9

Warning: This book contains sexually explicit content, which may only be suitable for mature readers.

Nate Tippie and Brandon Wilde are gay, single, and hoping to meet that special man, even though fate has not yet delivered him to their doorstep.

Nate's sister, Hannah, and her kooky BFF, Marilyn, are poised to help fate with that task by creating a profile on the gay dating site, OpenHeartOpenMind. They are only exploring, but when a face and body are needed for the created persona, they use Nate as the model.

When Brandon comes across the false profile, he falls for the guy he sees online. Keeping up the charade, Hannah begins corresponding with him, posing as Nate.

However, real complications begin when Brandon wants to meet Nate, who doesn't know he's being used in the online dating ruse. Hannah and Marilyn concoct another story and send Nate out to let the guy down gently. But when Nate and Brandon meet, they feel an instant and powerful pull toward each other. Cupid seems to have shot his bow, but how do Nate and Brandon climb out from under a mountain of deceit without letting go of their chance at love?

*For my good friend Ijeoma Ajibade, for her support of LGBT rights—and gay romance*

*We know what we are, but know not what we may be.*

—William Shakespeare (Hamlet)

# Author's Note

I just wanted to say thank you for reading my book. With every book I write, I need a reader to conspire with me to bring it to life, so I can't even begin to say how much I appreciate your spending time with my stories and using your imagination to help create something new where nothing existed before.

If any of the foregoing leads you to wonder if I am who I say I am, the answer is yes. No pen name, no authorial persona. I envy those who have enough imagination left over after they write a novel to create all that too.

I welcome hearing from readers and respond to every email I get personally. Feel free to write me at any time at rickrreedbooks@gmail.com. I'd love to hear from you.

Please visit my website at rickrreedreality.blogspot.com to find out more about my books and me.

Join me on Facebook at facebook.com/rickrreedbooks and on Twitter at @rickrreed.

# Chapter One

Brandon Wylde faced the form on his iMac screen with something akin to terror. Or maybe the emotion causing his mind to go blank and his heart to beat more swiftly could more rightly be called performance anxiety.

What was causing this fear of failure and quickened breath was the registration page for a gay dating website called OpenHeartOpenMind. Brandon had been all over the Internet, searching for a site that would put him in touch with other gay men looking for romance and the promise of something lasting and *not* for hookups. Now, there was no shortage of the former—the hookup sites were rampant, and as much as Brandon felt that "to each his own" was a motto worth living by, these sites were not his own. A close-up picture of an asshole (in the literal sense) or a hard dick might be titillating to some, but to Brandon it was simply a bore. How could one tell if one wanted to even "hook up" when seeing only a faceless body part? The idea gave Brandon the creeps. Did we have sex with genitals alone? No, we had sex with entire human beings, for Christ's sake. No matter how big and thick the dick was or how open and inviting the asshole (literal, again), Brandon couldn't imagine a meeting of any sort with simply a body part.

His "pickiness," as his man-whore friend Christian always said, was what kept Brandon alone and yearning at age twenty-nine. "Just go online. You can have a hot guy delivered to your door within an hour, like a pizza, a delicious, mouthwatering *pepperoni* pizza. Hold the cheese!"

Christian was no stranger to the embraces of many men, culled from sites like Manhunt, Adam4Adam, or Craigslist (or as Margaret Cho referred to it—the *Penny Saver* of dick) and, more lately, Grindr and Scruff. Christian swore by these electronic connections and, as far as Brandon could tell from their happy-hour conversations, took advantage of their charms on an almost daily basis.

Brandon shook his head and wondered if what Christian was shopping for online was more a fix than a human connection.

Brandon knew what he himself was, what he had, and the condition was incurable.

He was a romantic. As much as his hormones told him that all he really required in this world was a warm place to bury his dick, his more developed senses begged to differ.

Brandon wanted someone with whom he felt a special connection, someone with whom there was that magical spark he read about in the gay romance novels he devoured with increasing frequency, to fill the void missing in his life. Brandon wanted chocolates and flowers. He wanted love poetry. He wanted surprise weekend getaways to remote mountain cabins or quaint bed-and-breakfasts. He wanted someone to curl up next to on the couch, falling asleep together to some old black-and-white movie.

He wanted someone with whom he could share not only his body, but his life.

Christian told him, "You're never going to find the man of your dreams, unless you bring some of those wet dreams you're still having at your advanced age to life! Just get laid! No man's going to buy the merchandise without a free sample."

*Really, Christian? Really? And why are* you *still alone, then?* Brandon knew Christian spent almost all of his free time online. Hell, Brandon could even count on Christian to be on his phone, on Grindr or Scruff, when they were out to dinner or one of the clubs. Brandon would twiddle his thumbs with Christian nearby, oblivious and texting furiously, always on the prowl for his next hookup, who usually lurked somewhere nearby.

Why was the man never satisfied?

Brandon had a secret, one which he had never shared with anyone, especially Christian.

He was almost a virgin. He had only two pathetic sexual experiences on his résumé. First, there was an embarrassing, guilt-ridden "affair" back in high school that had lasted for all of two weeks (although Brandon wished for more). And the one time, back in college, when he had met his second paramour in the basement men's room of King Library on the Miami University (Ohio) campus. The guy wanted Brandon simply to kneel down between the stalls so he could blow him, but Brandon was far too fearful to engage in such an act and even then, he wanted more—like to see his cocksucker's face. Besides, Brandon wasn't even sure why the guy kept putting his hand under the stall, not knowing then it was a signal for him to kneel on the floor. So Brandon, romantic at heart that he was, simply grasped the signaling hand and held it.

This prompted his tearoom trick to flee the bathroom—and Brandon followed him outside.

Somehow, in the stairwell outside the men's room, Brandon convinced his bathroom suitor to take him home, to an off-campus apartment where the two young men quickly and furtively got one another off, worried about the imminent arrival of the guy's straight roommate.

That experience, sordid and unsatisfying as it was, left in Brandon a desire to chase windmills, if that's what his idealism could be called. Brandon was not going to settle. If he couldn't have the whole enchilada (the enchilada being a relationship that was satisfying not only on a physical level, but also on an emotional one), he wanted none of it.

Unfortunately for Brandon, he had come of age during a time when Internet and even smartphone connections made hooking up fast and efficient. Brandon conceded those connections might possess those benefits, but they were not for him.

He was interested in *both* of a man's heads, thank you very much. And he would not settle for less.

He believed a man who thought the same was out there. Somewhere.

Which is what brought him, right now, to the registration site for OpenHeartOpenMind. When he had finally landed upon the dating website, he was thrilled to find their mission statement on the home page, one that dovetailed with his own inclinations.

It read:

*We here at OpenHeartOpenMind believe in old-fashioned romance. If you're looking for impersonal, easy sex and lots of it, there are plenty of other sites that cater to your interests. Go for them.*

*OpenHeartOpenMind is for the man who wants to date, who knows that sometimes delayed gratification can make the rewards all the sweeter.*

*OpenHeartOpenMind is for gay men who think the road to love is paved not just with physical attraction (although we'd be lying if we said that doesn't play a big part!), but with mutual respect, shared interests, and the common goal of wanting more than just merging genitals, but merging hearts and minds as well.*

*Good luck on your dating journey!*

Below the mission statement were icons that urged the potential user to sign up and the current user to sign in.

When Brandon read those words, he quickly clicked on "sign up" because, in a way, he had already "signed up" for the very attributes the website promoted.

So now he began filling in the editable boxes on the site with his particulars: name, age, city and state: Seattle, WA, height: 6'1", weight: 198, body type: athletic. Brandon was nothing if not honest, so he quickly changed "athletic" to "beefy." He went on. Eyes: hazel, hair: dark brown, body hair: hairy, facial hair: full beard.

Brandon was relieved that OpenHeartOpenMind did not ask, as most of the other sites did, for his dick size or if he was top or bottom (although he definitely leaned more toward the former, but, as he had found, it was hard to top oneself).

Brandon came at last to the part where it asked for a headline and a short ad describing what one was looking for. And this was really the section that was giving him fits.

*How do you describe your heart's desire in 200 words or less? How can you just post what you hope to find in a man on the Internet for all the world to see? Can it possibly work? Is this really the way I want to meet someone?*

Thoughts like these crowded his brain, urging the more insecure part of himself to simply abandon the exercise. If he was a true, old-fashioned romantic, would he really be looking online for his true love? Wouldn't they meet casually somewhere, like a café or bookstore, where shy glances and almost covert smiles resulted in perhaps a quick conversation confirming that they might exchange email addresses, if not phone numbers? Or shouldn't they meet humorously, thumping melons down at the neighborhood Safeway? Or maybe by coincidence in, say, a fender bender at rush hour?

*You are just letting your performance anxiety get to you. This is 2013, buddy, and online is how it's done these days. Although it's certainly possible you could meet a man at the grocery store, Starbucks, or jogging on the trails that surround Green Lake, this way is much more likely to get some results. And even if it doesn't, what do you have to lose? This site is not costing you anything, except for maybe some time, and by doing this, you may just be aligning the universe to give you what you've been searching for.*

*As your mom always told you when you went off to school, when you went off for your first job interview, or your first date back in high school, "Just be yourself."*

Mom was right. He would just be his honest self, and the words would come.

## Down-to-Earth Honest Man Seeks Same

*I'm not looking for fireworks, just the potential.*

*I am a twentysomething guy, told I'm good-looking and in okay shape (kept that way not by eating right, but by logging twenty-five miles a week or so running). I have all my teeth and all my hair. My body functions normally for a twenty-nine-year-old. I don't have gas (well, not much).*

*I like horror movies, romantic comedies, and family dramas. I cry at the drop of a hat and laugh easily and am proud of both. I like classic jazz: Sarah Vaughn, Duke Ellington, Oscar Peterson. I love to read: gay romance, thrillers, and memoirs. I don't like sci-fi, reality TV, or selfishness. I will eat just about anything, but appreciate good food, good wine, and good restaurants.*

*I live in Seattle's Green Lake neighborhood, and if you can't find me at home, I am usually running around the lake—sometimes more than once.*

*The only thing I have that's incurable is a romantic heart. If you're afflicted with the same condition, maybe we're a match.*

*Want to know more? Ask me. I promise to answer...honestly.*

It took a little trial and error, and while Brandon didn't think he was going to win the Nobel Prize for literature, he thought his ad made him come off okay, or at least normal. More importantly, he was pleased he had captured at least the essence of himself. There was no pretense, so he was optimistic that whatever the ad might snare, it would at least be someone who knew him for who he was.

His final task was to upload a picture of himself. He opened the file of photos on his computer called, simply, "me," and began searching for just the right one. At last he settled on one that his mom—God bless her—had taken last summer, when the two of them had taken the ferry from downtown over to Vashon Island for a picnic on the rocky, driftwood-strewn beach. In it, Brandon squinted against the sun, with Puget Sound in the background. He was tan, with a little rose along the bridge of his nose and the tops of his cheeks, and he looked happy, his dark hair sticking up against a backdrop of a blue and cloudless sky. He thought anyone could see the hope in his hazel eyes.

He clicked on it to load it to the site, waited for it to appear, and then saved his profile. He got a message telling him it would post within a few hours, after moderator review.

*Well, here goes nothing*, Brandon thought. *Or, maybe, just maybe, if the timing is right, the stars are aligned, and I'm very lucky*—something.

# Chapter Two

The girls were a little drunk. But that was okay. It was Saturday night, and they were safe in Hannah's Capitol Hill town house near Volunteer Park. No one had to get up the next morning, and—since Marilyn had planned to stay over—no one had to drive later on.

Hannah and Marilyn had become friends when Hannah, laid off from Washington Mutual Bank in the economic downturn of 2008, had accepted a position at the front desk of Aloha Dog and Cat Clinic. Hannah, with her pixieish good looks, boundless energy, carrot-red hair, and welcoming smile, was an immediate hit with animals, clients, and veterinarians alike.

She was also a big hit with Marilyn, the *grande dame* of the five women who, in rotating shifts, manned the front desk of the busy veterinary practice. She had brought Hannah under her wing, taking it upon herself to train Hannah on the practice's computer system, end-of-day cashing-out procedures, billing, scheduling, filing, and how to deal with fractious cats, overly amorous dogs, and demanding owners.

The women had become fast friends and now spent almost every weekend together. As their time together expanded beyond the employee lunchroom and the pair began going out for happy hours, movies, and shopping excursions to discount outlets like T.J. Maxx and Nordstrom Rack, they became almost inseparable.

Then they found they had a shared interest: gay men.

Marilyn, with her dyed-black hair, cat-woman glasses, rose-tattooed shoulder, and penchant for all-black attire, was the first to bring up the topic. It was back when Hannah came in the employee lunchroom to find her reading a gay romance, a genre that Hannah, in spite of having a live-in gay brother, Nate, had never heard of.

"What are you reading?" Hannah sat down with her Tupperware container of lettuce, radishes, cucumbers, and tomatoes, and proceeded to squirt some homemade lemon tahini dressing atop the salad.

"*Chase in Shadow*," Marilyn had replied, displaying the bright-red cover with a close-up of a handsome blond man. Marilyn had returned to her reading, taking quick bites of her Subway sandwich. "I love me some hot man-on-man stories, especially ones like this one with so much angst!"

Hannah had not wanted to interrupt, but she was intrigued. The cover model's blue eyes had snared her. "What's it about?"

Marilyn looked up, smiling patiently, and told her a quick summary of the story of a sexually confused young man and his forays into attempted suicide and gay porn in his quest for true love.

"So it's a gay book?" Hannah shoveled a forkful of what her brother called "rabbit food" into her mouth.

"What is that? Like when one book is attracted to another book? They hook up by entering through the back cover?" Marilyn snorted with laughter.

Hannah rolled her eyes. "You know that's not what I meant."

"Sure, I guess so. Although it's more popularly known as m/m, or male/male, romance. You've never heard of it? I thought Nate was gay."

"He is; he is. But he doesn't read much. I didn't know you had an interest in this sort of thing."

"Well, honey, I've been reading 'this sort of thing' for quite a few years now and, let me tell you, there's a ton of good stuff out there. Take your pick from hot, sexy man action or sweet romance, you can find it. I dunno—I've always been a huge romance fan, but I was getting bored with the hetero stuff. And then I stumbled on m/m and became a huge fan." Marilyn shrugged. "I think maybe I like the power dynamic of two guys falling for each other. It's usually more equitable. It's certainly hotter." Marilyn winked. "More dick!"

After she was finished with *Chase in Shadow*, Marilyn loaned it to Hannah, and she had, without trying, brought a new reader into the genre. That first loan led to many more, and soon both of the women were contemplating attending GayRomLit Retreat, the big gay romance fan convention held every year, so they could meet and fawn over their favorite authors.

But tonight, at this impromptu sleepover at Hannah's, the girls weren't reading. They were drinking, gossiping over their coworkers at the clinic, and despairing about their bad luck in the romance department.

Hannah envied her brother his good fortune. She said, "My brother! He needs a welcome mat in front of his bedroom door and maybe one of those turnstile thingies in the entrance, you know, like they have at admission gates?"

Marilyn cocked her head, a twinkle in her dark-brown eyes. "Nate's gettin' a lot?"

"Oh Lord, sometimes I think he brings a different one home every night! I never know who's gonna be at the breakfast table next morning! And if he isn't out on the prowl at the bars, he's in his room, on his damn laptop. Apparently, finding guys online, at least for gay men, is as easy as rolling off a log."

"Or straddling one," Marilyn quipped. "Straddling and sliding down on it slowly." She got up to demonstrate, pantomiming straddling and then inching down on something large—and delicious—testing the endurance of her black stretch leggings, which sent both of the women into gales of snorting, hysterical laughter.

The girls were more than a little drunk.

After they had wiped the tears from their eyes and reined in their mirth, Hannah said, "Let me show you." She got up unsteadily and moved to the dining room, where her own laptop sat in permanent residence on the table. She unplugged it from the wall and brought it back over to the couch, plopping down next to Marilyn. "You should see some of these sites he goes to! And the pictures. Girl, get ready to have your hair curled."

Hannah's fingers flew over the keyboard while Marilyn looked on. Soon they were gazing down at the opening page of Manhunt. A gorgeous shirtless man smiled out at the two women, welcoming, and the home page told them that there were more than 60,000 men online at that very moment.

"That's more dicks than at a convention of Richards!" Marilyn screamed.

"I think my brother has tried every last one of them," Hannah said, which sent them both into howls of laughter again.

Marilyn refilled their wineglasses. "Can we see some of the guys?" She leaned close to the screen, almost as though she was waiting for one to pop out of the screen.

"I shouldn't do this," Hannah whispered. "It's really an invasion of privacy. But we can't see much unless we log on. And my brother, God bless him, uses password1981 for almost everything. I bet he does here too. He already told me his user name. How could I forget a name like BottomFeeder69?" Again, the women hugged each other, laughing.

Marilyn confessed, giggling, "I might have peed a little."

Hannah chose to ignore Marilyn's admission and resisted the urge to run to the hall closet for a towel and spot remover. "Should I do it? Sign us in?"

"Why not?" Marilyn slurred. "He's not due back anytime soon, is he?"

"Nah," Hannah said. "It's Saturday night. We may not see him until the morning."

"Then let's see us some hot mens!" Marilyn leaned forward, eager.

"Girl, put your tongue back in your mouth," Hannah said.

Hannah typed in the user name and password she was pretty sure would be the keys to the man kingdom, and just like that, she was in.

Disneyland might be the magical kingdom for children and wholesome families, but Manhunt was the magical kingdom, apparently, for gay horndogs. Hannah and Marilyn scrolled through page after page of tiny thumbnail photos of men in various stages of dress—and arousal. Marilyn gasped at a close-up of a huge dick, next to a beer can to demonstrate relative size, a rivulet of come leaking down its shaft. Marilyn gasped, "Good God, woman! They're allowed to post shit like that?" Marilyn looked away from the photo, and then back again, and then away, and then back once more. She gasped when she saw the headline for the beer can guy was "Looking for a Husband."

"Yeah, right," Marilyn snorted. "With a pic like that, I'm sure he attracts the serious-minded fellas in droves."

Hannah found the opposite of beer can guy a couple pages over. Here was a photo of a guy in what looked like a red Columbia GORE-TEX jacket. He was cute in a burnished, outdoorsy sort of way, with light-brown, medium-length hair, a scruffy beard, and a sweet smile. He posed in front of a range of snowcapped mountains.

"Ah, here's one even a girl could fall in love with. Isn't he just adorable? Puppy dog! A guy you could bring home to Mom..."

And then she looked at his ad headline, which read, "Into the five F's (in order): Fingering, Fucking, Fisting, Felching, Forgetting." His ad described him as an "insatiable pig" and "sometimes toilet" who enjoyed being "used and abused."

"Oh my!" gasped Marilyn, looking over at Hannah. "What's felching?"

They hopped over to Google and typed in the term. When they saw what it was, both women unleashed uncomfortable titters, clutching each other for support.

Hannah clicked out of Manhunt. "I think we've seen enough."

Marilyn said, "Aw, come on. We didn't even see your brother's profile."

"And we're not going to. I decided before we even invaded his account that I would not look at anything tied directly to him, like reading his messages."

"We could have read his messages?" Marilyn wondered. "That might have been eye-opening. Let's just take a lil' peek. It'll be educational."

Hannah shook her head. "No. I couldn't do that to Nate. Living with him is about as up-in-his-business as I want to be."

Hannah and Marilyn were getting tired and quiet as the hour grew late and the wine they had drunk began to have a soporific effect. As they both gazed into the pillar candle flickering before them on the coffee table, being lulled by the trancelike music of Moby, Marilyn wondered, "Are they all like that?"

"What? Gay men?"

"No, silly. The sites—where gay men connect. I mean, that one was so out there, so focused on sex alone. I've posted and gone online looking for love myself, but all the ones I've been to are usually more about dating, common interests, stuff like that. Look, I'm not judging or saying we're all not looking to do the nasty, but with the straight sites—at least the ones I'm familiar with—there aren't pics of spurting dicks, or God forbid, wide-stretched va-jay-jays. Usually, it's just your run-of-the-mill headshot. And let me be clear—by head shot, I mean facial close-up.

"I just wonder if there's a gay equivalent. You know, a place where gay men look to find someone to maybe go out to dinner with, rather than eat for dinner." Marilyn shrugged. "A place where a gay man can find another man to just date. You know, like back in the olden days."

Hannah slurred, "Where's the fun in that?" Then she laughed. "Just kidding."

"Doesn't Nate date?"

Hannah giggled; it was time for her to get to bed. "Nate. Date. You're a poet and don't know it." Then her face grew serious as she pondered her friend's question. "Gee, now that you mention it, I don't know. Date? I don't think so." Hannah grew quiet for a moment, frowning.

"He has lots of sex. He has guys over all the time, which I wish he wouldn't because most of the time he doesn't know these men from Adam." She snorted. "Or Adam4Adam."

Marilyn gave her a quizzical look.

"It's another gay hookup site."

"Oh."

"But Nate going out on a date? I can't remember the last time." And Hannah felt suddenly sad for her brother. It seemed his life was all climax, with no foreplay or buildup. She wondered if all the nameless sex got to be boring, or if he would laugh at her for wondering.

"Wow. Okay," Marilyn said. She could see the look of sadness on Hannah's face and didn't want to take things about Nate any further. Sure, all those hard dicks could be a lot of fun, but what about when you just wanted to talk to someone, share your bad day or your good day, enjoy a meal together, open presents on birthdays or Christmases? Didn't Nate miss that?

Marilyn went back to her original question. "So, are there gay dating sites? You know, like where guys talk about more than dick size or if they're tops or bottoms or versatile or whether they're into groups." Marilyn snorted. "Or *felching*. Good Lord!"

Hannah shrugged. "I don't know. I can ask Nate when he comes home."

Marilyn snagged Hannah's laptop off the coffee table. "Or we could find out ourselves." She moved her finger over the mouse pad to wake the computer and then went to Google, which was still an open tab. She typed in "gay romantic dating sites."

Immediately, Google returned with a predictable host of results, many of them more of the same, a la

Manhunt. But the search also led them to About.com, which had an article that listed gay dating sites, where one could meet someone for a sandwich of pastrami or turkey, rather than a sandwich a man might make with a Latino and a construction worker with him as the filling.

"Look at this, Hannah. There are gay dating sites, after all. Here's a whole list of them." She angled the laptop so Hannah could see.

"Let's take a look at one of them. I bet you as soon as we get in, we're gonna see hard dicks, coming dicks, assholes stretched as wide as—well, I don't know what— the Texas sky?"

"Oh, don't be such a cynic," Marilyn chided. She clicked on the hyperlink for one that caught her eye: OpenHeartOpenMind.

The pair leaned close together as they read the mission statement positioned on the home page. Together they looked at the collage of happy male couples, all clothed, doing things like hiking along alpine trails, biking, toasting glasses of wine over a candlelit table, and, of course, the classic cliché of walking hand in hand along a beach, roaring surf and setting sun in the background.

Hannah said, "I think we can safely say that, yes, there are gay dating sites. Even ones that are romantic. Look at all the soft-focus crap. Why, it's almost G-rated."

"Should we take a look?" Marilyn asked, moving the cursor around on the home screen, searching for an icon that would open up a tour or show her who might be "online now."

But there was no such thing.

"Looks like the only way you can get into the site is if you create a profile," Hannah said, thinking that would put an end to the matter. Thoughts of snuggling under her down comforter were becoming more appealing as the hour grew later. She felt fuzzy-headed and fatigued after all the wine.

"Well, we could do that."

"Do what?" Hannah asked. And then it dawned on her what her friend was suggesting. "Oh no, I don't want to travel down that path. That's dishonest."

"We'll just create it for tonight, so we can have a look at this different breed of gay men—a kinder, gentler homosexual. You know, as opposed to the ones who are interested in breeding some hole or being a come dump." Marilyn found herself quoting Manhunt again.

"I don't know," Hannah said.

"Oh, come on." Marilyn chided, digging a finger into Hannah's side, tickling. Hannah slapped her hand away.

"Oh, all right! But you have to do all the work. I am in no state to create some online profile."

"Okay. Just help me out with the questions." Marilyn clicked on the sign-up icon.

They both surveyed all that would be required of them. Because Hannah was exhausted and wanted to make things go quickly, she suggested they use her brother, Nate, as their model for the online man they were building. That way, they wouldn't have to stretch to use their imaginations, and it would help keep things straight, so to speak.

So they filled out the personal data with everything about Nate, who was thirty-four, with sandy hair, blue eyes, and an athletic build. They put in their own Capitol Hill zip code. They said he was "naturally smooth" when it asked about body hair. They gave Nate the screen name of Whos2Know because they thought it was an oh-so-clever reference to their antics.

And then they came to the ad.

Hannah said, "Just put 'Lookin' for love in all the wrong places.'" She wanted to be done with it. She stared longingly at the stairs opposite the living room.

"Oh, come on. This is just getting interesting." Marilyn sat for a moment, quiet and pensive, and then her fingers began flying over the keyboard. She would pause, type, pause again, and then return to her task. When she was done, she set the laptop on Hannah's lap.

"Not too bad for someone who's a couple sheets to the wind, eh?"

Through bleary eyes, Hannah looked down at the ad that Marilyn had composed, all ready to be sent into cyberspace with the click of the "post now" button below it. She had to admit, Marilyn wasn't bad at marshaling her faculties even under the influence. This guy sounded nothing like Nate, but he did, however, sound like someone she'd like to meet. In fact, Hannah thought, he sounded a bit like *her*.

### Looking for Love in All the Wrong Places

*Okay, here goes. I'm coming up on my midthirties, and I have yet to meet that special guy. I am beginning to wonder if he's even out there. From my searches of the bars, other online sites, and even places like parks and beaches, the cynic in me is beginning to be convinced he's not.*

*So here's my last-ditch attempt. Are you like me? Maybe a little lonely? Maybe a little hungry for someone to add some spice, but also to add some sustenance to your life menu? I'm looking for a guy who wants to share the good and the bad stuff, who wants to cuddle up under a blanket and watch an old black-and-white movie while a storm rages outside, who wouldn't mind a hike up a mountain trail on a crisp autumn day, who wants to laugh together, eat together, share the hopes and dreams of the other—who wants to be one. The one.*

*Hello? Are you out there? If a nice-looking and nice man is out there with the same kind of things on his mind, hit me up. This is Seattle, so we'll do coffee first.*

Hannah looked at Marilyn, seeing a side of her she never knew existed. "Not bad at all. I'd love to see what you'd come up with sober."

Marilyn waved her away. "It would probably be way worse." She leaned forward eagerly. "Should we pull the trigger, then?"

"Aren't we supposed to upload a photo?"

"You have one of Nate on here?" Marilyn giggled, tapping the laptop's screen.

"Yes, I do. And no, we won't." Hannah thought this would be just what Nate needed, even more men vying for his attention. "It says that a photo is optional. Let's just leave it."

"Okay." Marilyn sounded disappointed. But it would be crossing a line for Hannah to post a picture of her brother to go with some imaginary online profile. "So shall we go ahead and post it?"

"Why not?" And Hannah reached over her friend to click on the icon that would post their ad. They were immediately told their ad would be live within the next few hours, after approval.

"And we're in!" Marilyn laughed as a welcome screen came up, and, indeed, they could see who was online now. They specified they wanted to see ads only from Seattle metro and that they wanted ads that included photos.

Immediately, a page full of ads with thumbnail photos came up, along with their ad copy next to them.

"Aw, look," Marilyn said. "It's like going on that PetFinder site. You just want to bring one home."

The guys on OpenHeartOpenMind were a world apart from the naked and erotic ones they had seen earlier. These guys, for one, were all clothed. Tank tops were about as scantily clad as it got. And, predictably, those favoring that item of apparel leaned toward body builders. But most of the guys on here looked wholesome, clean-cut, with big smiles and eyes that met the camera's lens, and thus the viewers. Some of the men were in close-up, others full-body shots, either somewhere around the city or in one of the many green spaces surrounding it. The men were dressed in suits and ties, T-shirts and jeans, athletic wear. There was even one dressed in a suede welding coat, plying his trade, sparks flying. Of course, being Seattle, even this relatively wholesome site had more than its fair share of men with tattoos and piercings. In Seattle, Hannah had once remarked (though not at the animal hospital) one could not swing a cat without hitting someone with a tattoo.

It was kind of a relief not to see a picture of a mouth with come dribbling out of its corners or an ass being penetrated bareback.

OpenHeartOpenMind left something to the imagination, something to be *found*. It was refreshing.

They read through dozens of ads, united by a common theme. These men were all over "the bar scene" or "online hookups." They all sought a serious connection, something with a potential for partnership, fun, and yes, romance.

Hannah was about ready to tell Marilyn she was going to head to bed before she began snoring right there on the couch when she spied a profile that not only caught her eye, but clutched at her heart.

It was the young man's picture that first forged a connection with her. There was something so joyous and winsome in his expression that she was immediately drawn to him. It was as though their eyes connected. It wasn't just his attractiveness (a little on the scruffy side) that made her want to pinch his cheeks, it was the spark in his eye that promised laughter, fun, someone who cared.

*Good Lord, girl*, Hannah thought, *you are not even falling for a gay man on some dating site. Uh-uh. You have seen enough fawning, desperate women fall all over your brother, thinking they can somehow catch his eye. It's sad. Pathetic.* But yet, she couldn't help it. This person, what was his name? Brandon. This Brandon's eyes had made a connection with her own. She read his ad and could see in it a true heart calling out to another.

Hannah suddenly felt bad for what they were doing. It was as though she and Marilyn were making fun of these men, who really were looking for the one thing everyone seeks in his or her time on the planet— meaningful connection.

"See something you like?" Marilyn teased, making Hannah wonder how long she had stared at this Brandon's photo.

"What? Oh no! Just tired. Staring at the back of my eyelids, just about." She stood. "I'm going to go up and get in bed, if you don't mind." She leaned down to kiss her friend's cheek. "The guest room's all made up. Go up when you're ready."

"Thanks, hon. I'm just going to play around in "Gayland" here for a few minutes, if you don't mind."

"Just erase that profile when you're done. We don't want to get anyone's hopes up."

"Or anything else." Marilyn snickered. "Our guy sounds pretty cute."

Hannah thought of her brother, Nate. "He is. See you in the morning." Hannah started up the stairs and then stopped.

No telling what trouble Marilyn could get into on that computer. She didn't know if OpenHeartOpenMind had an instant message function, but if it did, she could imagine the kind of discourse a drunken Marilyn might initiate. The woman was not shy, and Hannah thought with a shudder of some of the shocking things she might say, especially when cloaked by a veil of anonymity.

*Better safe than sorry.* Hannah backtracked down the stairs and stood before her friend, who looked up and away from the screen after a moment. "What?"

"Would you mind?" Hannah tugged at the top of her laptop. "I want to take this upstairs with me." Hannah thought fast. "I like to check my email before I go to sleep."

Marilyn's carefully tweezed eyebrows came together in suspicion. "You don't trust me, do you?"

"Oh now, it's nothing like that." *It's everything like that, honey.* "I'm telling you the truth."

Marilyn, a little angry, slammed the lid down on the laptop. "Fine." She held it out to Hannah. "I don't know why you can't check your email on your phone, like everybody else."

Hannah said, "Screen's too small." Then, to try to appease Marilyn, she said, "We can look at this more in the morning. Okay?" She turned and picked up the remote from the coffee table and offered it. "Here. Watch some TV if you're not tired yet."

Marilyn's eyes lit up. Hannah could just about see the lightbulb click on above her head. "Your brother got any gay porn?"

Hannah rolled her eyes. "I'm sure he does." Because she was tired and didn't want to argue, she ran up the stairs to Nate's room and took a quick look around. There, on his dresser, was a DVD case that showed a white man sitting astride a black man's large cock. The movie had the charming title, *Rectum Wreckers*. Marilyn would love it.

She came back downstairs and handed it to her friend.

"Oh my God!" Marilyn shrieked, delighted.

"You know how to work the DVD player?" Hannah didn't wait for an answer. She had watched enough movies in that very room with Marilyn at the controls to know the woman did. Although the cinematic fare they had enjoyed together in the past was nothing like what she had just brought downstairs. The idea of watching gay porn caused a queasy wave in her stomach.

Obviously, it did not have the same effect on her friend, who had already greedily torn the disc from its case and was headed toward the DVD player.

"Have fun. See you in the morning."

"G'night," Marilyn mumbled, paying Hannah absolutely no mind.

Upstairs, Hannah shed the jeans, T-shirt, and fleece she had worn, letting the clothing fall to the floor. She could get it in the morning. She went into her en suite bath and quickly brushed her teeth and smeared some moisturizer on her face. She grabbed her flannel nightgown from its hook on the back of the bathroom door and slid into it.

She crawled into bed and switched off the light. As soon as she did so, though, she began thinking of their foray into OpenHeartOpenMind. She should probably delete the account before it caught the attention of some poor guy, or worse, Nate, although she didn't think he cruised such wholesome online communities.

She threw back the covers and grabbed the laptop, then took it back to bed with her. Powering up, she saw that the site was still open, and she—or Whos2Know—was still online. A blinking icon at the screen's top told her she had mail.

"Oh Lord," she whispered, "Already?"

She opened the OpenHeartOpenMind system email. It was from the site administrator, welcoming her to the community and telling her the profile was now live. "And this is how we get into trouble," Hannah said, searching for where she could delete the account.

But then a pair of lovely hazel eyes and dark hair and beard drifted, unbidden, into her consciousness. Brandon. She knew it was simply the wine making her think about him. After all, he was gay, right? In the morning she would laugh over her brief infatuation with the guy.

But right now, it wouldn't hurt to take one more look at him, would it? She went back to the profiles and located his. She clicked on his picture to make it bigger and smiled, then stroked the screen (and his face) with the tip of her finger. She could imagine he was right there, in bed with her. "You're such a cutie," she said to the picture.

"Why aren't there any nice straight boys out there like you—for me?" she wondered to Brandon. But if he knew, he wasn't telling.

Perhaps it was the wine, perhaps it was the late-night hour, perhaps it was both of these things, but Hannah, in that moment, threw caution to the wind and did something she would have not expected from herself. From Marilyn? Yes, maybe.

She clicked on the icon on Brandon's profile that said Email.

When the screen where she could compose her message came up, Hannah shook her head. Inside, she told herself there was no point to what she was contemplating. For one, it was futile. For another, it was cruel.

But his damn eyes kept coming back, haunting. She just wanted to see what he was like. She would leave it alone after one message. If he wrote back, she promised herself, she would not respond, but would close out the account, as she had planned.

She started typing.

*Dear Brandon,*

*I do hope that's your real name. So many guys on this site use cutesy names, myself included, instead of telling us who they actually are. I admire you for using your own name. I like that honesty.*

*I admire you for other things too. Your eyes, which caught and held mine. Your ruddy skin, your dark hair and beard. The way you seem to be laughing in your photo. It looks to me like a nice, easy laugh—one that would never be cruel.*

*Tell me about the picture. When was it taken?*

*Where? Who was the photographer? He must know you very well, because not only do you look good in the picture, something of your soul comes out as well. I imagine a very kind soul.*

*Ah, you probably think I'm a nutcase. But I just wanted you to know your picture and your simple ad touched my heart.*

Hannah's fingers hovered for a moment between the Trash icon and the Send icon, and in the end, she felt compelled to hit Send.

She wouldn't respond if Brandon wrote back.

She wouldn't. Really.

She fell asleep hugging her computer to her chest.

# Chapter Three

Nate shifted himself gingerly, trying not to awaken the guy snoring next to him. He angled his ass to the edge of the bed, on his side, and took in the sleeping stranger's countenance. He looked to be about forty, with tight dark-brown curls, olive skin that was most likely Mediterranean in origin, and a big nose. His mouth was open, and, judging from his snores, Nate surmised he probably didn't need to worry about waking him. A line of drool ran from the corner of his mouth down his cheek. The scent of alcohol perfumed the air.

Nate got himself up to a sitting position, casting one more glance over at his latest "relationship." He had met him the night before at Charlie's, an unassuming little neighborhood gay bar, still on Capitol Hill but away from its gay epicenter on Broadway. Charlie's was on Fifteenth Avenue, sandwiched between a coffee shop and a vintage clothing store, just down the street from the Safeway.

Their drunken gazes had connected in the mirror hanging over the bar. Once Nate had sent the guy a beer, it wasn't long before Nate was following the guy back to this very apartment, a run-down studio in the attic of an old house on Seventeenth.

He couldn't recall what the guy's name was, or if, indeed, they had ever exchanged names. It didn't matter. The guy had fallen asleep with Nate's mouth on his half-erect cock and had yet to rouse—or become aroused.

Silently, with the grayish light of a summer's dawn filtering in through half-drawn miniblind slats, Nate dressed, thinking of that old Peggy Lee song, "Is That All There Is?" which pined, in a bluesy way, for something *more*.

Nate wanted something more. More than one-night stands with strangers. More than online hookups that could sometimes result in good sex but never went any further. More than a job, even though the one he had helped him pay his share of the expenses on his sister's town house a couple of miles away. He had yet to share his town house with anyone else. He didn't know why. His occupation, taken up on a whim, had spiraled out of control, making him someone he didn't even know, in spite of his success.

But what he really wanted was someone to wake up next to who was not a drunken stranger, sleeping one off.

He hoped to one day wake up to a smile, to familiarity.

He was thirty-four years old, and what did he have to show for it? He lived as a roommate with his sister. His last boyfriend, an English major he was certain he'd spend the rest of his life with, had been when he was in college in Eugene, Oregon. He had a job, but again, it was a secret occupation, and it was kind of an independent contractor sort of thing, so he had no healthcare, retirement plan, or any other benefits. Nor did he have the camaraderie of going into an office, which he imagined would be staffed by a quirky cast of characters akin to the one shown on the TV show, *The Office*. His love life, such as it was, was a string of men who, while some were hot in bed, were all commitment-phobic.

Nate had managed to slide into his jeans and hooded sweatshirt without waking his slumbering counterpart. He moved aside a pile of clothes that lay on a bedside chair to sit and put on his socks and Nikes. *You're dressing like a kid. Maybe that's part of the reason you have a kid's life...still.* He supposed, at one time, he was just as commitment-phobic as the men he met online and in the bars. How was he to know he'd wake up one morning—and perhaps it was this very morning—and realize he wanted *more*? Life's little epiphanies lived by no man's schedule, Nate thought.

As he was snagging his keys from the glass-topped nightstand next to the bed, the sleeping guy awakened. He snorted and smacked his lips. Had Nate heard a fart? Their eyes met in the shadowy room, and the sleepy man rubbed his eyes and gave Nate a grin. He rolled onto his back and whipped the covers off his prone form.

"You want a taste?" He nodded down at his erection, rising up from a nest of black pubic hair. It might as well have been a carrot rising up from between his thighs, for all the appeal it had for Nate at the moment.

"Thanks, man, but I got to get going." Nate started toward the door, wondering if this was the first time the sight of a naked cock, aroused, had not whetted his appetite. What parallel universe had he awakened in, where he would turn down such an offering? But he just wanted to go home, to get into his own bed, sleep for a few hours, and then maybe see if his sister, Hannah, was interested in Sunday brunch.

At the door of the bedroom, Nate turned to mouth the insincere words so common at the ends of such meetings—about having a good time the night before, about how he'd call, maybe they'd get together soon.

He was surprised to see the man on the bed had raised his hairy legs, pulling them back almost to his shoulders, his hands positioned in the crooks of his knees. "Maybe you'd like a taste of this?" Nate swore the guy's asshole winked at him.

Nate chuckled. "Tempting as that is, I do have to get home."

"Married?" The guy lowered his legs, spit on his hand, and began stroking himself.

"I wish." Nate hurried from the apartment, nearly tripping over an orange tabby cat that had stationed itself near the front door. It yowled a goodbye to Nate as he exited.

Outside, Capitol Hill was, for a change, quiet. Nate glanced at his watch and saw it was only a little after six. The August air had a chill to it, with a hint of morning-dew dampness. It was all very pleasant. Nate decided he would walk home and revel in the quiet, trying to avoid the feeling that he was the only person awake in the world.

*

When Nate rolled out of bed four or so hours later, the sun was streaming in his bedroom window as he sat up, stretching. He loved Seattle summers and the fact that they were the Emerald City's most closely guarded secret. The uninitiated believed it rained all the time there, but the fact was, there were fewer places that had more perfect summers than Seattle, with long strings of days with abundant sunshine, low humidity, and temperatures that hovered in the upper seventies during the day and dropped to cool, comfortable upper fifties and low sixties at night.

He felt well rested and, although that was a good feeling, it made him wonder if he was past his expiration date for sleeping comfortably with another person. He knew he could never have gotten the kind of rest he'd just had with his one-night stand from the night before. What was his name?

*Buddy, you never knew. Don't kid yourself.*

Nate went downstairs in a pair of flannel sleep pants, black-and-red checked, and a Rat City Rollergirls T-shirt.

"My! My!" Marilyn screamed from the couch. "How do you fall out of bed looking so gorgeous, Nate?"

Nate smiled and went over to kiss his sister's best friend on the cheek. "Flattery like that could just about make me turn, sweetheart."

Marilyn pushed him away. "Yeah, yeah. You and me both like a nice big cock too much for that to ever happen."

"Marilyn!" Hannah chided.

"Well, it's true," Marilyn said, sipping her coffee.

"It's also true that I just had a bowel movement, but I didn't feel compelled to share it with you all until now." Hannah went into the kitchen, where she poured her brother a mug of coffee and brought it back to him. "You up for brunch? Marilyn and I were just talking about it. Portage Bay in South Lake Union?"

Nate took a sip of his coffee, savoring. His sister knew just how he liked it: three sugars and a generous dollop of half-and-half. Pancakes at Portage Bay, extra-sweet, extra-creamy coffee, and probably a healthy amount of maple syrup sealed the deal for Nate for two reasons. One, it would make him happy. Two, he would need to run the trail around Green Lake that afternoon.

Twice.

And he actually liked to run. It was like meditation for him.

"Sounds heavenly," Nate said, looking out the window at the perfect summer morning. "Just me and my girls. Everyone will be jealous."

"Sweet talker," Marilyn cried. "You get lucky last night?" Before he had a chance to answer, Marilyn said, "Look who I'm talkin' to. Stupid question. Was he cute? Did he have a big dick?"

"Marilyn, I swear, sometimes I wonder if you are a gay man trapped in a straight woman's body. The things you ask! And yes to both."

Hannah curled her feet under herself on the couch and asked a question Nate thought would more rightly come from a straight woman's mouth. "Will you see him again?"

Nate winked. "I don't know. Anything's possible." *As in, yes, I could pass him on the street or bump into him again in one of the bars, or even online.*

Marilyn got up from the couch, being careful not to spill the coffee in her mug as she stood. "Time to make myself pretty." She looked Nate up and down. "Unlike some people who shall remain nameless, girlfriend here has to work at it a little."

Nate watched her ascend the stairs.

Hannah asked, "So was the guy you met last night nice?"

Nate turned to her, unable to force a smile onto his face. "I wouldn't know." He followed Marilyn up the stairs, calling down to his sister, "Give me fifteen."

*

Nate should have known better than to run the trails at Green Lake on a sunny Sunday. He fought against rollerbladers, bikers, gaggles of young moms with strollers, couples holding hands, other runners and walkers, and even swimmers who spilled from the lake's two beaches. It was hard to get into any kind of stride when every few minutes he was dodging a bicycle or jumping over a pair of leashed dachshunds.

But there were perks to running around Green Lake on a summer's day—eye candy. As crowded as the popular lake was, it was crowded too with any number of handsome young men with lean, fit bodies, doing exactly what he was. The bonus was that most of them, like Nate, were shirtless. Their muscles stood out, glistening, defined by a semigloss coat of sweat.

There was a certain sexual tension in the air.

He had passed the dark-haired man once before, since he was running the opposite direction from Nate. Their eyes had met, and Nate was struck by the intense hazel color of the other man's irises. The flecks of gold in his eyes were almost hypnotic. And he had a beard that Nate could suddenly *feel* chafing against the tender skin of his neck.

The man's long, lean body, fur covered, and the absolutely fierce pace he was able to keep up, in spite of the crowds all around, also struck Nate. What was the guy doing, anyway? Sub-seven-minute miles?

After drinking all last night and then indulging himself with banana-walnut pancakes and bacon this morning, Nate was lucky if he was maintaining a pace of ten or eleven minutes per mile.

Even though he wasn't running as fast as the other guy, Nate still grinned, knowing in the brief moment of eye contact he had been mutually admired. It was funny how much could be learned in one flirtatious glance, passing someone else. The language of the eyes was so much more eloquent than the one of the tongue. Eyes spoke honestly and without inhibition. This guy's lovely orbs, for example, told him that this handsome, dark-haired stranger was gay...and that maybe, just maybe, he was interested. Straight men did not hold a glance as long as two gay men did. Why, it was practically an art form.

Now, as Nate pushed himself to complete the three-mile circumference of the water's edge, he wished he had seen the guy again. Perhaps they could have talked, exchanged numbers, maybe gotten together later to compare running tips, to get to know one another. To have sex? Nate chuckled, slowing at a pier near the aqua theater and walking out on it to stretch. Well sure, he thought, surprising himself, but there was something about this guy, the openness in his eyes, that made him think of the possibility of something more.

Nate looked around from the vantage point of the low, wood-slatted pier and saw no one who looked like the dark-haired young man he had passed earlier. *Isn't that always my luck?*

Nate pulled one of his calves against the back of his thigh, searching for that perfect dark-haired man. Because their encounter had been so fleeting, Nate was able to ascribe all sorts of wonderful characteristics to the guy—things like a quirky sense of humor, a love of books, an insatiable sexual appetite, a capacity for kindness and compassion, a love of nature—that may or may not have been true.

He brushed some sweat from his forehead, his hopes of seeing the dark-haired man once more thoroughly quashed.

Besides, didn't Quentin Crisp, one of Nate's literary heroes, once claim there was no "great dark man"? It was only an illusion, something unattainable, yet something for which we hunger nonetheless.

# Chapter Four

Brandon stripped out of his running shorts, Brooks shoes, and socks and headed to the shower. As much as he loved to run—it was almost Zen for him, like meditating—this was his favorite part: when the exertion was behind him and he was headed for a long, luxurious, muscle-loosening hot shower.

He adjusted the spray just a notch below scalding and winced a little as he stepped under it. But soon his body adjusted and the heat felt good, as if his muscles were butter, cold but softening, melting. He soaped himself up slowly, thinking of his run and the blond he had made eyes with as he coursed around the water.

Green Lake was not the cruisiest spot on the planet, or even the city of Seattle—it was far too family oriented for that—but Brandon had had his share of ten-second love affairs along its circular course. You know, the ones where you'd make deep eye contact with a guy, holding it for longer than what would be considered appropriate, perhaps even adding in the flourish of a head swivel and neck crane, to watch the retreating features of one's temporary beloved. *That* was a ten-second love affair. They were okay, but Brandon was more in the market for love affairs of the ten-year variety.

Today, the blond had been his respite from his long six-mile run. He was gorgeous, smooth where Brandon was hairy, blond where he was dark, yin to his yang. And there had been an undeniable connection when their gazes locked, enough to make Brandon certain he wasn't mistaken that the guy was interested.

Brandon had even waited around in the parking lot by the aqua theater, hoping he'd see the blond again, maybe have the courage to approach him, but there was no sign of him. All that passed by him was a gaggle of teenage girls, all busy on their smartphones, not one of them paying the least bit of attention to the other.

"Story of my life," Brandon said to himself, stepping out of the shower and reaching for a towel.

After drying off, running a brush through his damp hair in an attempt to tame it, and dressing in a pair of old sweats and a mangled, plain red T-shirt that should have been thrown away years ago, Brandon sat down, barefoot, at his computer. It had been a couple of days since he posted his ad on OpenHeartOpenMind, and he had yet to get any serious nibbles, leastways ones he was interested in reeling in. There was the guy from Tacoma who sounded nice until he revealed he'd love to see a picture of Brandon's feet. "I'm not weird!" he had promised. "I'd just love to see your feet bare or even in socks, if you're modest." This comment had been followed with a smiling and winking emoticon. Then there was the guy in Madison Park. He seemed like a good sort until he revealed his need for discretion, because he was on the "down low."

Brandon shook his head as he signed in to his account, wondering if he was doomed to never finding anyone special. Perhaps there was no one special out there. Was it possible the market had simply dried up? That all the good ones were taken?

He'd had high hopes for this dating site when he'd read its mission statement. But so far, OpenHeartOpenMind offered more of the same. Although its pictures and come-ons were tamer and more vanilla, the site had not distinguished itself from its more in-your-face brethren. At least on Craigslist, you wouldn't be duping yourself into thinking Prince Charming was hiding behind the glory hole he had set up in his apartment.

As the site booted up, Brandon told himself to be patient. Patience had never been one of his virtues. He thought microwaves took too long.

"It's only been a couple days," he said to the air.

He was pleased to see he had five new messages. Three he deleted immediately because they contained attachments that turned out to be pictures of his correspondents naked and aroused. One guy was even kneeling on his bed, pulling his ass cheeks apart, as if to say, "Come on in; the water's fine."

"Please." Brandon clicked on delete again and again. "Have you heard of Craigslist?" He peered a little closer at the pic. "What is that? A hemorrhoid?"

The fourth was from someone who did sound nice—a guy who worked on the Microsoft campus out in Redmond as a technical writer. He was cute in a nerdy sort of way, slim, with tortoiseshell glasses and straight brown hair that looked like it would have the habit of falling over one eye. But his note to Brandon, detailing the technical writer's likes and dislikes and how he'd been looking forever for the right guy and the fact that he mentioned he had so little time with all of his twelve-hour days, ultimately turned Brandon off. How was he to build a relationship with someone who worked such long hours and, really, showed no inclination to slow down the pace to meet someone special? Priorities!

No, a workaholic was not what Brandon wanted.

He got up, rooted around in the fridge, and sat back down with a can of Diet Coke.

He almost deleted the next message, since he saw one of the cardinal red flags on any online personal ad: there was no photo uploaded. The absence of a photo could indicate that the guy wasn't out (which Brandon had no interest in), that the guy was playing games, or that the guy was, not to put too fine a point on it, ugly.

Yet Brandon was inclined to at least give the guy a chance and read his message, especially since he had struck out with the other messages in his inbox this morning.

With low expectations, he opened and began reading—and was charmed with the man's honesty, with his sincere hope to make a meaningful connection and, Brandon had to admit, with his flattery.

Brandon was all set to move on to browsing the online hopefuls and to send out some of his own messages, but he thought this guy deserved a response. Straightforwardness and honesty were qualities he admired in a person, and this guy seemed to have them in spades. Sure, the lack of a photo indicated he probably looked like the love child of Phyllis Diller and Gilbert Gottfried, but he seemed like a nice, down-to-earth guy. Even if he did turn out to be someone he would come to kiddingly call "Gramps," he could end up being a friend. And one could never have too many of those.

Brandon hit the reply icon and began typing.

*Dear Whos2Know,*

*First of all, what's your name, anyway? We'll never get anywhere unless we know who the other is. Yes, Brandon is my real name. Last name, Wylde, like Oscar, although not spelled the same. Also, like Oscar, I can resist anything but temptation.*

*And no, I don't think you're a nutcase. What came across to me in your email was a nice guy, someone I'd like to get to know better. I do wish, however vain and shallow this makes me sound, that you had uploaded a picture to go with your profile. It's not just because I want to see if you're hot or not (although I'd be lying if I claimed differently), but it also helps me to have a face in mind when I write to someone. If you don't want to upload a profile pic, you do know you can upload one and mark it as private, don't you? Then all you'd have to do is unlock it so I could see. I'd love it if you'd do that for me.*

*Now, about my picture. It was taken on Vashon Island last summer, and the photographer was not, as you guessed, a he, but a she. Okay, okay, I am not a closet case with a girlfriend, but a gay boy with a mom who loves him. I like the photo because it was a happy day for the two of us, and my mom, as you said, knows how to capture emotion with her camera. And I bet I know what's on your mind, so I'll calm those suspicions right now—yes, I am a mama's boy.*

*And proud of it. I'll save the unabridged version for later, but my dad left us when I was about four, and it's been me and her against the world ever since. She has shown me what real love and unselfishness are all about. So if that makes me a mama's boy, I have no problem with it at all.*

*About me: I work downtown for a big law firm, writing marketing copy for them and maintaining their website and corporate blog. It's boring work, but it pays the bills on my Green Lake apartment. I'm just steps away from the water, and I love running on the trails there. A perfect summer night for me is just sitting out on my balcony with a glass of wine at dusk, watching as the sun gradually makes its getaway and the lights across the water begin to come on. When I'm not outside, I love good movies, good food, good conversation. I have a passion for horror in the first, Thai in the second, and inquiring minds in the third.*

*And I'd love to hear from you again. I got on this site because I'm ready—you know for what.*

*Are you? So, what's your name, anyway?*

Brandon proofed his note one final time, thinking it showed off who he was and seemed friendly without being overly flirtatious or desperate sounding. Why should it, anyway? He did hope to meet a man, but he wasn't desperate.

He hit Send, and his heart lifted a little in anticipation. He had a good feeling about this. But one thing he knew for sure. This thing, whatever it was, would go nowhere fast if Whos2Know's next missive didn't contain two things: a picture and a name.

Without those, there couldn't be any possibility for a relationship, even a friendship.

He shut his laptop, wanting to wait to hear back from Whos2Know before exploring the site any further. His phone rang. He thought it might be his buddy, Christian, who would want to go out to the Cuff's Sunday Tea Dance, but Brandon didn't think he was in the mood for that right now. He was relaxed and settled at home.

But it wasn't Christian calling; it was his mother, Nancy. He looked down at her face on his phone screen and wondered how he had bypassed all the angst other people his age had gone through with their parents and found a mother who could be a good friend. Maybe it was because she looked young enough to be an actual friend, a contemporary. She appeared to be about thirty, even though she was coming up on forty-eight, with a clipped blonde bob, sapphire-blue eyes, a kind of big nose, and a smile that made everyone want to smile back. His mother was like liquid sunshine, but she was, as anyone who knew her could attest, not all sugar—there was a lot of vinegar mixed in. There had to be. It took a lot of strength to raise a boy alone, especially when you were dumped by your husband at twenty-two.

Brandon pushed the screen to connect with Nancy. "Hey, Nan. What's up?"

His mother sighed through the phone. "Every time you say it, I regret my decision to let you call me by my first name."

"Okay, *Mommy*, what's going on?"

"Nancy, please. Lord, I also regret that I raised a smartass."

"I learned from you, *Mother*."

"I suppose that's true. And I have to admit I'd be disappointed if you weren't a smartass. Some of the best people I know are smartasses. The world would be a much bleaker place without a smartass or two."

"So, are you just calling to chat?"

"Well, yes. Am I keeping you from something?"

One of the good things about his relationship with his mom was that she was so cool about his being gay. He had come out to her when he was a junior in high school, when she had found an unfamiliar pair of tighty-whities in the laundry (Brandon owned only boxers, at least back then). When she had asked him whom they belonged to, no other thought rose to his mind other than to tell her the truth. "They're Jack's," he mumbled, rolling his eyes before casting his gaze downward. He could distinctly recall the heat that had risen to his face after the admission, akin to a flush of acid being injected under his skin. "He forgot them when he stayed over on Saturday."

His mother hadn't said anything for a long time. "Are you disappointed?" Brandon had asked, looking up at his mom, searching for condemnation in her eyes.

Nancy had said softly, "Yes."

Brandon's heart had done a little lurch. He had known and appreciated all the sacrifices his mother had made for him through the years. Although he was okay with the idea that he was queer, he hated to disappoint Nancy in any way. For more than just himself, he wanted her to be proud of him.

"I'm disappointed," she said, moving closer, finally sitting down next to him on their couch and taking his hand. "I'm disappointed because you're fooling around with a guy who wears such tacky underwear, son. Didn't I teach you to have more class than that? Good Lord, do you know how much bleach it took to get the skid mark out of the back of them? Yuck! Who is this jerk, anyway, that he forgets his own gross drawers?" Nancy had snorted with laughter, which caused Brandon to join in with a kind of giddy relief.

"But let me make it clear—I am *not* disappointed in you being gay. That would be dumb, wouldn't it?"

Brandon had looked at her, head cocked, not sure he got her meaning.

"That would be like me being disappointed that you have dark-brown hair or that you have hazel eyes. It would be like me being disappointed that you don't like beets—although I certainly don't get that: beets are delicious, and so good for you. But that's neither here nor there.

"So you're gay. So what? What else you got? You're my son. I love you. *You.* I don't want you to be any different." Nancy had given him a little kiss, right on the lips. "It's the oldest cliché in the book, but I mean it—I just want you to be happy."

That memory was just one of the many reasons he not only loved his mother dearly, but also thought of her as one of his best friends.

Getting back to her question about interrupting something, Brandon said, "Well, I have news."

"Go ahead."

"I placed an ad on one of those gay dating sites."

"Oh, Brandon, I don't know how I feel about that. Aren't those sites just about sex? Can't you meet a nice boy out running or at, I don't know, a gay bridge club or something? Don't they have queer softball leagues? Church groups?"

"It's not how you think, Nancy. This site is all about dating, about romance. You're from back in the olden days. Heck, you're still afraid to pay your bills online. Lots of people, couples you meet these days, met their significant others online. It's what people do. You get everything on the Internet."

"If you say so."

"Anyway, what I wanted to tell you was that I just got a nice note from a guy who seems really cool."

"What's he look like?"

Brandon hesitated. He knew his mother wouldn't like what he would say next. "That's just it. His profile didn't have a picture."

Nancy laughed. "Well, that can't be good."

"But his note was so nice, so genuine. He even complimented your photography. I used one of the pictures you took of me last summer on Vashon."

"But no picture? Honey, he probably has Charlie Manson eyes or he looks like a chimpanzee—or he's eighty years old. Not that there's anything wrong with that."

"I thought so too, Nan, which is why when I wrote back, I asked him for a picture. And if I don't get one, we won't be going any further. You need to know what a person looks like, right?"

"That's my boy. Shallow and all about the looks."

"Nancy! I just want to have a face in mind when I write to him again. And come on, you have to admit there needs to be some physical attraction in order for things to go anywhere. It would be lovely to think we lived in a world where only what was on the inside counted, but that's not the case, is it? By the way, how's that new hair color working out?" Brandon knew Nancy had just had her hair dyed a honey-wheat color, after she lamented how much gray was beginning to sprout on her head.

"No, you're right. I hope it all works out. It would be great to see you meet someone. Much as I love dinners out with you, going to plays and movies, hikes at Discovery Park, my son dating his mom isn't exactly what I had in mind for you."

"Right."

"So you want to come over for supper?" Nancy lived not far away, in the Ravenna neighborhood a little east of Brandon. She had scrimped and saved for years and had finally been able to afford a small cottage on the edge of Ravenna Park. "I'm making meatloaf."

His mother was many things, but a cook was not one of them. Meatloaf was her default, made with eggs, ketchup, and a packet of French Onion soup mix.

"That's nice of you, but I'm thinking I'm gonna stay in."

"Wait and see if this Mr. Wonderful messages you back?" Nancy chuckled.

"That's not it at all." But it was. "I just want to hang out here, wind down before the work week starts." Just so he didn't hurt her feelings, he added, "Besides, I've had a steak all thawed out since Friday, and I need to throw it on the grill."

"Well, okay, but stop by tomorrow. I'll wrap some meatloaf up for you and you can have it for sandwiches."

Brandon concluded his call with his mother with a promise to keep her posted on the online front and then hurried back to the desk he had set up in the corner of the living room.

# Chapter Five

"Have a good run?" Hannah asked her brother as he passed, the scent of sweat in his wake.

"Spectacular," Nate said, heading up the stairs. "Fabulous. Life-changing. If I could have only one run in my life, I'd want it to be the one I just had. It was chocolate ice cream, lobster tail, and an orgasm all rolled into one. It was unforgettable."

"I just asked."

"I'm off to shower. I thought I'd head out to the Cuff for the Sunday Tea Dance. Want to come with?"

Hannah didn't want to say it, but spending the afternoon and early evening in a bar with her brother was not her idea of relaxation. Despite having been alone for longer than she wanted to recall, she couldn't help feeling a little sad going out to gay bars, even though she usually managed to have a lot of laughs. But it always nagged at her. In such a social situation, her brother would almost always meet a man, while the opposite was true for her. "Nah. I want to just stay in. Take a bubble bath. Read that *Entertainment Weekly* I've been meaning to, answer some emails."

"Play some solitaire?" Nate chuckled.

"You're mean. I'm not mean to you."

"I just want you to come along; you make it more fun. If Marilyn were here, I bet you'd go."

Marilyn had left an hour ago, to go home to her cat, Mike. She had mentioned something about wanting to read a book by an author she had just discovered.

"If Marilyn were here, she could go with you—and would. That woman is cuckoo for the gays. I've said it before, and I'll say it again, she's a gay man trapped in a female body."

"And what's wrong with that?"

"Nothing—don't take it the wrong way. I just would like to go out with you sometime where there's a chance you're not the only one to get some cock."

"Hannah! My virgin ears! I don't need to hear that!" Nate bounded up the stairs.

Hannah called after him. "I'd be willing to bet my life savings that's about the only part that's virgin!"

Nate didn't respond. She listened as his bedroom door closed, then heard the hiss of the pipes as he began running water for his shower.

The real reason she wanted to stay home, though, was something she'd never admit to Nate. She wanted to check OpenHeartOpenMind to see if Brandon had replied to her email. She knew it was silly. There was no payoff in pursuing this, and there never could be.

She read and watched TV for a while, waiting for Nate to head out to the Cuff.

Once he left the room, she moved over to the dining room table, where she had plugged in her laptop to let it recharge, and logged on to OpenHeartOpenMind. She felt a little tingle as she signed in with her screen name and password, feeling a certainty that Brandon had written back to her.

*Slow down there, sister. If he has written back, you need to remember it's not to you. It's to your fantasy guy. Right, right. You think I don't know that?*

She let out a little relieved giggle when she saw there was a message from Brandon. Hungrily, like a starving woman, she ate the message up, devouring it in big bites, not pausing for punctuation.

Why, he sounded just as cute as he looked! A truly nice man, to use that overused descriptor, but it summed up this Brandon so, well, nicely. Again, Hannah wondered why there was no straight equivalent of Brandon out there for her. A little voice in her head chided her that if she was, say, on Match.com, she might have a lot more luck finding the straight Brandon than she would on a gay dating site.

The truth was, Hannah had done her fair share of online man shopping and had, sadly, always come up with defective merchandise.

She read Brandon's message over again, wondering how she should respond. He had asked for a picture. He had asked for a real name. Maybe she should finally do what she had promised herself and Marilyn the night before—delete the account. It was the right thing to do, before things went any further. How did the saying go? Oh, what a tangled web we weave, when first we practice to deceive?

But she knew she wouldn't delete the account, in spite of her conscience telling her she should. She wanted to talk more to Brandon. What was the harm in that? She listened to her brother clomping about upstairs, knowing he was throwing different clothes out on his bed, trying to find just the right ones to allure and seduce. Hannah was fairly certain her brother wouldn't be home tonight or, if he was, he wouldn't be alone. God only knew who would face her across the breakfast table come Monday morn.

She wondered briefly how her brother managed to have so many late nights out, when the rest of the world had to take into consideration getting up for work early most days. He worked from home, that was true, but what he did continued to be a bit of a mystery. She had pressed him once, and he had hastily—and none too credibly—told her he did underwriting reports for large life insurance policies, interviewing applicants and getting the lowdown on their personal and professional habits so the insurance underwriters could give a thumbs-up or a thumbs-down on the policy. But, as long as he paid his share of the rent and bills, who was she to question? He certainly *did* spend a large amount of time on the computer, yet she rarely heard him make any phone calls. Wouldn't that be a part of the interviewing process?

Whatever. Brandon awaited her.

She sat at the table, once more drinking in his handsome face as she wondered how she could keep him hooked, so to speak. Could she go on another site and grab a picture of a stranger? Could she snag a stock image off a photography site? It just didn't seem right.

The idea came out of nowhere, it seemed to Hannah, although she might later admit to herself that it had been buried in her subconscious since she and Marilyn had created the online profile.

Why not use a picture of Nate? After all, he was who they had modeled the profile after, so the picture would match in all the important details. Plus, she had scores of pictures of her brother right on this very laptop's hard drive. Grabbing one would be a cinch. Grabbing a good one would also be a cinch. Her brother photographed almost insufferably well. And why shouldn't he? He bore more than a passing resemblance to film star Bradley Cooper.

*But no, Hannah, you can't use Nate. He lives right here—in Seattle. What if, God forbid, this Brandon should run into him out at one of the bars or something?* Hannah thought that was unlikely. Brandon, her Brandon, simply did not seem like a bar person. *Oh, what does that mean? What is a bar person, anyway? He's young, he's single, he's looking—he probably goes out sometimes.*

Just for the hell of it, she opened her pictures folder and found one dedicated to a trip she and Nate had taken one day last spring. The two of them had both been off on a weekday, and she had convinced Nate to go with her to Golden Gardens Park, over in the Ballard neighborhood. The day, she recalled, had been unseasonably warm and sunny, after weeks of misty gray. She remembered that she just couldn't bear the idea of being cooped up at the vet's office all day, so she had roped her brother into playing hooky with her.

They had strolled the park's wooded trails, where the shadows offered a cold, bracing contrast to the bright sunlight.

They had ended up on the beach, and it was there Hannah had snapped a few candid shots of her brother, with the startling blue of Puget Sound behind him and the Olympic Mountain Range, its peaks still crowned with snow, almost seeming to rise up out of the placid water.

The sunlight had hit his strong features just so, as he looked off into the distance and the clear blue waters. A breeze lifted his hair off his forehead. It was lovely, made all the more so because Nate seemed completely unselfconscious, as if unaware of his picture being taken.

Without giving herself a chance to censor or second guess, she quickly uploaded one of those photos to her profile for OpenHeartOpenMind. If Nate saw it, he probably wouldn't think twice about it. Lord knew the man had so many online profiles out there already. If he did see it, he'd probably assume he'd put it there himself. And if Nate ran into Brandon and an awkward conversation ensued—who knew? Maybe it would be the start of something special for her brother.

She ignored the pang of jealousy this thought caused her and began typing a response to Brandon.

> *Dear Brandon,*
>
> *Thanks for getting back to me so quickly. You know what? I already love hearing from you. I find myself eagerly looking forward to the time when I will open up my laptop and find a message from you, like a present under the Christmas tree. Is that too hokey? Maybe. But I have to confess—I can be a little sentimental.*
>
> *Okay, so you ask and you shall receive.*

Hannah bit her lip. She had uploaded Nate's picture. Should she give him Nate's name? Doing so would cross a line, and her brother might be very upset with her. Hell, an invasion of privacy like that might cause him to be enraged. And if not enraged, the alternative would be worse. He would see her as unbalanced—a little touched in the head, as Marilyn might put it.

In spite of these very reasonable thoughts, she decided she *would* use his name. If she used it, along with his details and his picture, she thought it would be okay if the men ran into each other in the real world. A little confusing, maybe, but if she knew her brother, he would simply think Brandon had seen one of his many online profiles.

The logic—and her plan—had holes big enough to drive a Hummer through, but maybe because Hannah wanted to keep things as simple as possible, she stuck with her plan. She continued writing.

*My name is Nate. Short for Nathan. Rhymes with date, mate, and late, which I sometimes am, punctuality not being one of my strong suits.*

*And here I am, in the photo you asked for. Like you, this one was also taken by a female family member, my sister, whom I adore. She's a pretty cool lady and absolutely thinks the world of me, which is great, because I feel the same about her.*

*I hope you like what you see!*

*So tonight, I am just lounging around the house. I just got the new Criterion Collection transfer of* Rosemary's Baby *on Blu-ray, and I'm looking forward to watching it in all its pristine glory, as it looked when it was first released. I've seen it a bunch of times, starting with when I was way too young to watch a movie about a woman being raped by the devil. Thanks, sis! In a bit, I'll probably call up the neighborhood Thai joint, order up some green curry, and bring it back home. Lazy Sundays are the best, aren't they?*

*So, what's your story? How did you end up working in a law firm? Please don't tell me you have aspirations that way. I don't know if I could abide a lawyer—or a Republican. What's your favorite color? What's your favorite playlist on your iPod? Boxers or briefs? What do you like to do in bed?*

Hannah thought she'd end on that note, a little flirty, a little shocking, and she really did want to read the answer to that final question so she could picture Brandon doing it. But not with her brother! Lord, no!

She hit Send.

# Chapter Six

Brandon didn't see Nate's reply until Monday morning. He had fallen asleep in front of the TV the night before, watching an old episode of *The Walking Dead* on DVD. When he awakened around midnight, groggy and with a crick in his neck, all that had been on his mind was collapsing into bed.

But now, in the morning and refreshed from a good night's sleep, the first thing on his mind was—had Whos2Know written? And, more importantly, had he revealed who he was? Uploaded a picture?

He was like a kid on Christmas morn. He skipped his usual routine, hurried to his computer, and logged on to OpenHeartOpenMind. He laughed out loud when he was saw there was a message from Whos2Know. There were several others, too, but this was the only one that seemed to matter.

He looked first at the picture. He was a man, after all, and men were visual creatures. He couldn't blame himself for his biology, even if his mother would say he was shallow.

The picture—Brandon swore—caused his heart to still for just a moment, then to speed up rapidly. He shook his head, transfixed. After sucking in a breath, he whispered, "My, my."

Not only was the guy gorgeous, just his type, because Brandon was partial to blonds, but there was also something about him that touched him in a familiar way. It was as though he had seen him before. Had he? Brandon racked his brain, but even though the déjà vu feeling persisted, he couldn't recall ever having met this handsome specimen before. Brandon eyed the photo and liked that it was taken outdoors, liked the faraway look in the guy's eyes as he stared across serene sapphire waters that pretty closely matched, if the picture was accurate, his own irises.

He was beautiful.

But who *was* he?

Brandon dove into his note and saw that he was Nate. Nate, a nice simple name. Brandon said it aloud a couple of times, liking how it felt in his mouth. He glanced at the picture again, and his skin prickled as he thought he'd like the feel of something else in his mouth. "You dirty boy!" he whispered, chuckling.

The note was sweet. It appeared Nate really did want to get to know him. And from the way Nate had described his Sunday, it also looked as though the two of them might have a lot in common.

Brandon glanced up at the clock. He had slept a little later than usual, and if he was going to squeeze in three miles this morning, breakfast, and a shower, he had to get moving. The express bus downtown was due a few blocks away in just over an hour.

The logical plan would have been to wait until he got to work to reply. He could somehow make the time, but Mondays were usually his most hectic days, because the law office partners and associates respected no weekend boundaries, and he knew there'd be a ton of emails to wade through.

He didn't think he was monitored at work, but going on a site like OpenHeartOpenMind in the office was probably not the best idea.

*Just a quick note.* He began writing.

*Nate!*

*I am so glad I have your name, and even gladder I have a face to put it to. And what a face. Boy, you make my heart speed up. You make me think nasty thoughts. Sorry, but it's true.*

*I don't have a lot of time—hectic Monday morning and I have to be downtown soon for my job. As I mentioned, I work as a copywriter and webmaster for a large law firm. Yes, boring. But I have been there almost eight years, and I'm comfy. The pay's not bad, the benefits pretty good. No, no trust-fund baby here. Raised by a single mom in decidedly unluxurious, but loving, circumstances.*

*Let me just go through your questions real quick, and then I'll wrap up with a question or two for you. Favorite color: blue—like your eyes. iPod playlist—I don't know what my favorite is, depends on my mood, but since I listen to my iPod most when I'm running, I like the high-energy stuff, so I would say my disco playlist or maybe Lady Gaga. If I'm mellow, I like the old jazz masters—Duke Ellington, Sarah Vaughn, Oscar Peterson. What else? Oh yeah, boxers all the way. My boys like their freedom.*

*And what do I like to do in bed? You naughty boy. I'm not going to answer that, but will instead adopt the voice of a bratty schoolgirl and say, "That's for me to know and you to find out."* (Here Brandon inserted a smiling and winking emoticon.)

*My questions for you—first, answer all the ones you asked me, and second:*

*When can we meet?*

*Brandon*

Brandon laughed, delighted with his own boldness, but Nate, even with this brief note, had made him feel happy, excited, optimistic. He hit Send and knew he'd never be able to follow his own commonsense advice to stay off OpenHeartOpenMind at work today. He knew he'd be checking every hour or so to see if Nate had written back.

Brandon scrambled now because he had taken too much time on the note. He donned his nylon running shorts and a tank, gulped a banana down in about three bites, slid into his running shoes, grabbed his keys and iPod, and headed out the door, energized, for his morning run.

He was fast, buoyed up by the day's promise. Would he meet Nate soon? When? Where?

He wondered as he entered the lakefront trail, the morning mist nipping at his calves, where had he seen Nate before?

# Chapter Seven

Hannah needed this break. The vet clinic had been a horror sideshow this Monday morning, what with a full slate of appointments and surgeries, and things like a German Shepherd with a rubber and rope chew toy in its belly thrown in just for good measure. Lunch would have to be short, but still, it was a blessing—a chance to put her feet up and eat one of her favorite lunches, a peanut butter and strawberry jam sandwich, a bag of potato chips, and an apple. She felt like she was back in elementary school, and that, as Martha Stewart might pronounce, was a good thing.

Or at least not a bad one.

And the tiny employee break room was also blessedly empty, giving Hannah time alone with her thoughts.

She needed to think.

What to do about Brandon? He wanted to meet. Hannah wanted to meet him, too, but she had a feeling he might be disappointed he'd been corresponding with a creature that had an innie when he preferred outies. She felt a little pang of guilt, but also a hopeless desire to meet the man.

Maybe she could tape down her breasts, slap on a fake moustache, stick a sock in the crotch of her pants, and set up a date, hoping she'd pass. She could lower her voice a couple of registers, no problem. She giggled. The idea sounded like some kind of farce. She glanced down at her prodigious rack and thought that no amount of tape could tame those two.

Dressing up as a man was out, because passing as one was patently absurd. Hannah was all girl.

Still, she hated to draw things to such an abrupt close with Brandon. She wished he hadn't asked to meet so soon. But she had to admit to herself that it was a logical and not unforeseen request. After all, people did not sign up for these sites to make pen pals; they wanted to meet someone.

She would miss Brandon. *Unless...*

Marilyn interrupted her thoughts as she waltzed into the lunchroom, bearing her "ironic" *Dark Shadows* vintage lunch box in one hand and her iPad in the other. She eyed Hannah. "Have we ever had such a hellacious day?"

"I don't think so."

"I was afraid that Miss Pussy Galore out there was going to scratch my eyes out. They should bar that cat from the clinic. I swear, she's gonna kill somebody one of these days. And all just because of a little mani-pedi. For Christ's sake." Marilyn laughed and sat down. She pulled out a small Tupperware container of what looked like hummus, a pita round cut into triangles, followed by a bag of baby carrots and cherry tomatoes.

Hannah eyed her repast. "Healthy today."

Marilyn shrugged. "I need to lose ten."

Hannah thought Marilyn had been saying she needed to lose ten pounds since they met, and that was years ago. That ten had yet to go missing. In fact, it probably had another twenty to keep it company. Marilyn's lunch today looked low calorie, but the Top Pot maple bar she had eaten earlier that morning probably had packed a full day of calories.

Marilyn sighed and put her feet up on the other chair. She took a pita slice out, dipped it in the hummus, and began nibbling. She opened her iPad and tapped it.

"New book?"

Marilyn turned to Hannah, her eyes bright. Hannah had obviously pushed the right button. "Yes! Yes! And a new author—I don't know how I didn't know about this one before, but I discovered her last night browsing around on Amazon."

"Who?" If Marilyn didn't know about this author until last night, Hannah was sure this new find wouldn't ring any bells with her. Still, Marilyn's excitement piqued her curiosity.

"BF Mann. Honey, she is the real deal."

"Gay romance?"

"Yeah, but so much more. She has several books about this pair of gay private eyes, right here in Seattle. The twist is they're a father and son team."

"Both gay?"

"Yes! Isn't that the best? Anyway, they investigate all these kind of paranormal cases, and they act as each other's sounding board in the romance department. The other twist is that the son, who's in his twenties, is very happily married, and it's the forty-something *papi* who's on the prowl and who can never seem to meet the right man, though Lord knows it isn't from lack of trying. This dad is a girl of easy virtue, okay? But his sex scenes? Smokin'!" Marilyn sang out the last word and then laughed. She tapped her screen a couple of times. "Take a look." She positioned the iPad so Hannah could see the book cover for *Rampage*, which showed the Seattle skyline at the bottom, with a pair of hot men breaking out of the darkness above. Predictably, one was older, yet still the type Nate would refer to as a hot daddy, and the younger was kind of sweet. Thankfully, neither was shirtless, which would have been, to Hannah, a little creepy, since this was supposed to be a father and son.

"I'll have to pick up a copy."

"You need to get yourself a Kindle. I've told you. I can loan you books if you do. This one included. This BF Mann has this whole series, then a bunch of standalones, all gay erotic romance. She's a great writer, and it's cool reading stuff set here." Marilyn busied herself with the iPad for another moment and then shoved it toward Hannah once again. "That's her website."

Hannah looked down at the face of a smiling woman with spiky red hair and pince-nez, peering out at the camera. "BF Mann," the banner across the top read, "Not Your Mama's Gay Romance..." The woman looked like someone's kooky grandmother and not a gal who dabbled in writing about anal sex and things—and guys—that go bump in the night. Hannah shoved it back. "You'll have to tell me where to start with her. I have to finish this Josh Lanyon book first, though."

The pair was silent for a while, Marilyn reading and Hannah savoring the last of her potato chips.

Finally, Hannah said, "I hate to bother you when you're reading, hon, but I have a confession to make."

Marilyn slammed shut the iPad's smart cover, and Hannah heard the click of the device falling asleep. "A confession? *Pour moi*? Do tell! And I promise to absolve you of anything, honey. But I have to hear what it is before I dole out penance."

Hannah rolled her eyes and drew in a breath for courage. "I feel kind of weird admitting this, but remember when we signed up on that online gay dating site? You know, the romantic one?"

"What was it called? OpenMouthOpenHole?" Marilyn snickered.

"C'mon, I'm trying to be serious here."

"Yes, I remember." Marilyn narrowed her gaze. "What did you do?"

"Oh, something stupid." And she told Marilyn everything, including how she had given Nate's first name and uploaded his picture. "And now I don't know what I'm going to do. This Brandon wants to meet me, er, him."

"Well, it's obvious, sweetie. You have to shut this show down. Drop the curtain. Lights out. Show's over. Now." Marilyn took the leavings from her lunch and dumped most everything into the trash, then returned to load her now-empty Tupperware back into her lunch box. "I mean, what else can you do?"

"You're right; you're right." Hannah stared down at the table, tracing patterns in its faux wood-grain surface. She felt embarrassed and, oddly, sad. She would miss Brandon.

Marilyn was snickering.

Hannah looked up. "What?"

"You. I can't leave you alone for five minutes. Look what you get yourself into. Your life is a situation comedy, girl."

"It's not funny." Hannah thought of Brandon, of the warmth that came through in his notes. Maybe she could admit the truth to him? Tell him she was a woman pretending to be a man? Ask him if he'd consider being friends? Oh right, she was sure that would go over just swell. She sighed. "I just hate to delete the account and leave him hanging. I felt like there was a connection between us. It seems cruel."

"Honey, are you living in the real world? There may be a connection, but there is no 'us.' That poor guy has a fantasy man in his head, not you."

"I know." Hannah wished she had never traveled down this path. She wished she had listened to her own sensible inner voice for once in her life, the one that told her to delete the account she and Marilyn had created as soon as they were done checking out the profiles.

Marilyn interrupted her thoughts. "Well, there is one other option. Or a few, actually. The first is probably the more sensible. You could create a story where 'Nate' has to move away suddenly or something. Maybe a job promotion or he goes into the military—that could be hot. I don't know. You're the storyteller. That way, you could talk to him a bit more. Or even be a pen pal!" Marilyn chuckled. "Or how about this? An ex-love comes back in the picture, and 'he' wants to give it another try."

"I don't know." Hannah did know. Marilyn talked sense, but she didn't want to shoo Brandon away like that. She looked over at her friend. "You said a few options."

"Well, I'm actually kind of shocked you didn't think of this one yourself." Marilyn stared at her, waiting for several seconds. "Come on. It's as plain as the freckled nose on your face."

A lightbulb switched on above Hannah's head. "No," she whispered. She clasped her hands over her mouth, unsure if she was holding in a giggle or a scream.

"Having Nate meet the guy makes perfect sense," Marilyn said.

"He'd never go along." Hannah saw herself telling her brother what she'd done. She couldn't imagine he'd take the news happily. At best, he'd think she was a complete and utter nutcase with way too much time on her hands.

At worst, he'd be furious at her for appropriating his identity as she had. No, she could never tell him.

Marilyn scooted her chair a little closer. "I think Nate might actually like the idea. That boy loves nothing better than meeting men, right? And this guy is hot, isn't he?"

Hannah pictured Brandon's spiky dark hair, his beard, both of which contrasted so wonderfully with his hazel eyes. "Oh yes, beautiful. Girl, I look at him and I need a tissue...and not for tears."

Marilyn snickered. "Well, there you go. Why would Nate be mad or upset if you set him up with a hottie? Honey, he'd probably get down on his knees and thank you." She giggled. "Then he'd get down on his knees for this Brandon. I know how he rolls!"

Hannah had to admit her friend *did* have a point. Nate might look at her a little strangely. Even she knew what she had done was toeing the line between sanity and cuckoo. But Marilyn was right—when had Nate ever turned away a chance to get with a hot guy?

Hannah couldn't deny the sharp pang of jealousy she experienced at the thought of Brandon and her brother together. Still, such jealousy was totally irrational. Brandon could never be for her. She knew better than anyone that gay men don't "change." They don't suddenly "turn" for the right woman.

In some of the books Marilyn had loaned her, the converse sometimes occurred, where a seemingly straight fellow would "turn" suddenly for a man, realizing out of the blue that he had been gay all along, or at least gay for one special guy.

Hannah had never bought that either. Brandon was not going to become straight for her.

Besides, maybe things would work out for Nate and this Brandon, who did seem like a super-nice guy. And would that be such a bad thing? This way, she could befriend Brandon herself and maybe do her beloved brother a giant favor. If all went well, maybe she'd play Cupid and hook her brother up with someone, finally, who would last.

Wasn't that all any of us wanted?

"I see the wheels turning," Marilyn said.

"I'm gonna do it," Hannah said, wondering if there had ever really been any other alternative. "Now, if Nate is willing to go along with it—that remains to be seen. But I'm gonna tell him. Tonight." Hannah grinned. A sense of relief and anticipation washed over her.

The door opened, and Betty Cope poked her head in. The woman was Donna Reed to the clients, with a cloyingly high, sweet voice that was overly solicitous and Sunday-school charming. It was all an act. "You two bitches need to get your fat asses back out to the front desk. You're not the only ones who get a lunch around here." She slammed the door.

"Bitch," Marilyn whispered.

"She's right."

Marilyn and Hannah gathered up their stuff, put it in either the trash or their lockers, and headed back into the breach, to do battle with beasts, both two-legged and four.

\*

That night, Hannah made Nate one of his favorite dinners. It was something their mother had served them, a concoction she'd had growing up in St. Paul, Minnesota—hotdish. Hannah thought the casserole was kind of gross—hamburger topped with a can of corn, a can of cream of celery soup, a can of cream of mushroom soup, and a layer of Tater Tots, followed by a generous covering of shredded cheddar cheese.

As she slid the casserole into the oven, she thought that at least it was easy, and she knew it would put Nate in a good mood, reminding him of the mother they had both adored and whom they had lost, tragically, to leukemia, just four years ago. On the way home, Hannah had bought a six-pack of Stella Artois in bottles and a loaf of crusty sourdough bread. She didn't bother with a salad because the casserole had everything, right?

She wanted Nate to be in a good mood.

When he returned from his run through Volunteer Park, Hannah smiled at her brother, drinking him in. His calves alone were swoon worthy. Good Lord, if he was straight, he'd probably have so many women vying for his hand in marriage, it would make her head spin. As it was, he had too many—Hannah thought—gay guys vying, but not for his hand. No, they were interested in parts farther south, and her friendly, outgoing brother seemed to have no problem accommodating them.

"Supper's almost ready. Go take your shower, and I'll have it on the table by the time you're done."

"What possessed you to cook tonight?"

"I don't know. Just thought it would be relaxing." Usually, the very last thing Hannah wanted to do when she got home from work was head into the kitchen and start preparing a meal. It just seemed like an extension of the workday to her. Besides, Nate was home all day, and he usually managed to throw something together for them—a salad, or burgers on the grill, maybe some soup or chili when it was cold. If he didn't cook, Hannah would order in Thai or pizza, the ubiquitous takeout options in Seattle.

"Well, okay. I'll be right down. Smells good!"

Hannah watched her brother ascend the stairs, admiring, in a sisterly way, how gorgeous he was. She couldn't imagine why he wasn't with someone. Did he *not* want to be? He talked enough, when the two of them fell into a reflective mood, about finding someone special, wanting to settle down with one guy, maybe get his own place, a dog, have other couples as friends. She knew, in spite of the steady flow of hookups, Nate longed for someone special.

Yet it never seemed to happen. Hannah had watched a parade of men pass through her brother's life, and it seemed that he—or they—were always too caught up in what might be waiting around the corner, rather than seeing what was right in front of their faces. How could one ever settle if he was always wondering if someone better might be waiting in the wings? She had seen her brother date so many guys who seemingly had it all: great senses of humor, good looks, stable careers, financial security, charisma—and yet, sooner or later, they all fell by the wayside. Then he would start the process over again a few weeks or months later.

Would her brother never be satisfied?

Maybe the universe planned for him to wait for Brandon. Wouldn't that be a kick?

Hannah laid the table with their multicolored Fiesta Dinnerware and linen napkins. She even lit the taper candles that adorned their dining room table but were seldom lit because Hannah and Nate favored eating in the living room, in front of the TV. The dining room practically glowed, and Hannah had to admit, junk food or no, the hotdish bubbling away in the oven smelled wonderful and, in a way, redolent with memory.

When Nate returned, barefoot and dressed in a pair of faded and ripped jeans and a tight Paul Frank monkey face T-shirt, he sniffed. "Man, that smells like—like home. You made hotdish? I thought you didn't like it."

Hannah grinned. She didn't understand her brother's passion for what was a lot of processed junk thrown into a casserole dish, but she was glad it made him happy.

And then she understood his passion—really—when she saw the tears he struggled to blink back. "It's funny." He started to speak and then stopped, pausing for several long seconds that made Hannah's heart go out to him. He blinked rapidly and then laughed. "It's funny how food can just bring her back. I always remember her making this for us as kids."

"Served with Kool-Aid! Well, mine probably can't compete with hers, even though I do everything the same." Hannah donned some oven mitts to take the casserole out of the oven and set it on a trivet on the table. She set a serving spoon down beside it. "Dig in."

Hannah waited until after dinner to bring up what she wanted to talk about. She didn't want to spoil her brother's enjoyment of the meal and its attendant trip down memory lane. She watched happily as he helped himself to three servings and downed a couple of beers.

He belched at the end of the meal. "You know, in some cultures, that's considered a compliment."

"Why, thank you," Hannah said, rolling her eyes.

Nate started to stand. "You did all the work, so let me clean up, okay?"

Hannah sucked in a breath; it was time to face the music. "Sit down. There's something I want to talk to you about."

Nate regarded her warily as he retook his seat. "Everything okay?"

Hannah grinned to show him it was, but inside, her heart thudded uncomfortably. She was surprised her brother couldn't hear it, the way it was hammering. *Calm down. It's not like you're confessing to murder or some horrible crime. Yes, what you did was a bit bizarre, but Nate has known you his whole life. It might be a little weird, but no reason to be so terrified.* In spite of these thoughts, Hannah was still just that—terrified.

"Oh, everything's fine. I'm as healthy as a horse, stable job, and so on and so forth."

"Well, that's good. So what's up? These 'we need to talk' kind of conversations usually aren't good news."

Hannah leaned over to pull her laptop toward her. She flipped its lid up and signed into OpenHeartOpenMind. While she was doing so, Nate said, "Now you really have me wondering."

"I just want to show you something." She brought up Nate's profile, complete with his picture and the ad she and Marilyn had composed. A picture was worth a thousand words. Wasn't that how the saying went? She screwed up her courage, took a deep breath, and turned the computer screen toward her brother.

He peered at it, eyebrows coming together in what had to be confusion. She could see him using the mouse pad to scroll down the page. He shook his head, glancing up at her quickly. He shrugged. "What is this?"

"It's your profile, silly."

"I didn't post this. I've never even heard of this site. How did you find this?" Nate looked disturbed. It nearly broke her heart. For a moment, she considered telling him she and Marilyn had just stumbled across it and she was in the dark about it as much as he was, but knew the fib would never withstand close scrutiny.

Hannah stared down at the table and said quietly, "I didn't *find* it; I posted it."

A short, bitter laugh escaped Nate's lips, yet he didn't sound amused at all. "You what?"

Hannah looked up at her brother, almost unable to bear the look of disbelief on his face. "Marilyn and I got a little tipsy the other night, and we were just fooling around online." She went on to tell him how Whos2Know had been born.

Nate shook his head. "You're fucking kidding me, right? Why would you do this? It's bizarre."

Hannah tittered, sounding on the verge of hysteria. The air felt tight in her lungs. Heat rose to her face, burning. Had she ever been this embarrassed? She was the older sister here. Shouldn't she have more sense? If there was any way she could simply stand and run from their town house, she would. Why hadn't she simply deleted the profile? Nate would have never known. "We just wanted to see some of the guys on the site. You had to create a profile to get access."

"So...you just decided to use me? And my picture?"

Hannah nodded. "Please don't be mad."

"I don't know what I am, Hannah. This is weird. I can't get my head around it. Is this what you and that Marilyn do when I'm not around?"

"I swear, this is the first time we've ever done anything like this. And it won't, I promise, happen again."

Nate stared at the profile. Finally, after a long silence, he laughed, an easier carefree chuckle than the bitter bark of earlier. "At least you chose a cool pic for me. This is very flattering. Not only does it make me look good, it makes me look deep, thoughtful."

"It's you, Nate."

Nate put his hand over Hannah's. "I don't get why you'd do this, Sis."

"I'm sorry."

"I forgive you. We'll forget about it. Okay?"

Hannah nodded.

Nate stood and began gathering plates from the table. "I think I'm going to head over to the Hill tonight and have a couple cocktails. Want to come?"

"Nate. There's more."

He set the dishes in the sink and came back, eyeing her, arms crossed over his chest. "What?"

She told him about Brandon, about their correspondence.

Nate laughed again. "So you've been posing as me and writing to this guy? Are you nuts?"

"Yes, I am."

"Let me see," Nate said.

"Click on the email icon," Hannah said, feeling numb.

She waited as Nate went through their short correspondence, looking up at her, then back at the screen. Thankfully, a grin played about his lips. "Well, at least you make me seem kind of charming. I'd go out with me." He clicked and then gasped. "And *he* is hot!" He paused, drawing his face closer to the screen. "Oh my God!"

"What?" Hannah wasn't sure she wanted to know.

"I've seen this guy before. Just the other day."

"You did?" Hannah felt a chill.

"Yeah. Yeah. Running around the lake. Oh God, he's gorgeous."

"Then you like him?"

"I don't know. We even cruised each other a bit. Small world!"

Hannah thought now was her chance. "So you'd meet him, then?"

"Honey, I'd like to do more than just meet him."

Hannah was relieved. Maybe this wouldn't be so bad after all. She couldn't deny the jealousy she felt as it seemed like things were heading in the direction of Brandon and her brother meeting, but at least it was a connection—and maybe it boded well for all three of them.

"No! No way! Not after you set this up." He shook his head. "It's too weird." He gave a mock shiver. "It feels kind of incestuous, like my sister pimping me out. I don't need that."

*No, you certainly don't,* Hannah thought but didn't say. "I just feel bad. You read our correspondence. I thought it would be nice if you met him, only to let him down gently. I hate to just disappear. That seems so mean."

"Believe me, Sis, stuff like that happens all the time. Guys never call. They don't email back. They don't return texts. It's an occupational hazard. He'll get over it."

She didn't want him to get over it.

Nate pulled the screen close. "He is a cutie. Damn."

"Please. For me. Just meet him. Once."

"I don't understand why you want me to do this."

"Would it surprise you if I said I didn't understand either?"

"After this, Hannah, very little would surprise me."

"So you'll do it? I'll set it up. You just need to show up. Hot date with a hot man. How bad is that? What happens after you meet is up to you guys."

"This is crazy." Nate rubbed his chin. "Okay. I'll meet with him, but just to 'let him down gently' as you say. And then you have to promise me you'll delete this profile. It's just too strange for me."

"Promise."

"Okay, then. I'm gonna get to these dishes."

Hannah stood and touched him on the arm. "I'll take care of them. You go have a good time. And again, I'm sorry." She looked at him, entreaty in her eyes. "Hug?"

"Of course." Nate gathered her in his arms.

Who knew what would happen next? All Hannah knew was that she couldn't wait for Nate to get out of the house so she could write to Brandon again.

Maybe they'd even instant message?

# Chapter Eight

Brandon was in front of his computer once more the next morning, before heading off to work. Lots of emails had accumulated in his OpenHeartOpenMind mailbox, but there was only one he was interested in, only one he'd truly hoped would be there.

It was.

Nate. "Oh, Nate, you wrote back, you wrote back!" he whispered to himself, delighted, clicking on the little envelope to open the message. He began reading.

*Dear Brandon,*

*You're right. We do need to meet. I had thought about drawing this email thing out. I have to admit, checking my computer for new email has never been so much fun. It's always a delightful surprise when I find a message from you.*

*Story of my life: so many guys I've met flare bright, then burn out as quick as a match—and not, I'm sorry to say, a match made in heaven. It's happened to me so often I kind of expected it from you.*

*I hope that won't be the case. One thing I admire so much about you is how down-to-earth you seem. Simple. But not in a bad way. Just real. You know what I mean?*

*Anyway, I toyed with the idea of sending you more questions to answer, so I could get to know you better.*

*But then I thought, Hannah, you can just ask him these questions when you face him across a table in a café or at a bar. Wouldn't it be nicer to have the visual and the voice?*

*And the answer to myself was—yes. Of course.*

*So, Brandon, sir, would you do me the honor of meeting me? I offer two options, depending on your poison of preference—stimulant or depressant. Option number one is meeting at a bar. I suggest Union, just off Broadway on the Hill. It's small, quiet, and we can talk. Beer is usually my potable of choice. The second is also close on the Hill—the Starbucks on Olive Way.*

*The first is a bit more like a date, the second more along the lines of two buddies meeting up, with bright lights and lots of people around. Caffeinated conversation.*

*I could also come to you if that suits you better.*

*I am fine with whichever way you want to go. I have a suspicion that just being with you will be enough.*

*I only hope you'll pick something—and soon. I am free most weeknights. Hell, I am free most days since I work from home, so shoot me a couple times that would be good for you, and we'll get something set up. And do pick a place. I have a pet peeve about indecisive men.*

*Take charge!*

*Hope to see you soon.*

*Yours,*

*Nate*

Brandon read the message over again. One, because it delighted him, revealing that Nate was smart and seemed to have a good sense of humor, a little wittiness that Brandon really liked. In the past, he had always gotten bad vibes from men who sent him one-line emails. *Wanna get together? What do you like? Hey!* Those guys bored him, turned him off.

This Nate seemed to have a personality, a mind.

The second reason he read the message over again was because there was something strange in there. Brandon wanted to make sure he hadn't misread. He moved his eyes across the passage in question once more. *But then I thought, Hannah, you can just ask him these questions when you face him across a table…*

Hannah? Who the hell was Hannah? And why would he refer to himself as Hannah? Brandon checked out the keys on his keyboard. Yes, the "a" and the "n" were also in Nate, but the other keys were nowhere near close enough for this to be a typo.

It was a bit of weirdness in an otherwise wonderful message.

He wondered if Nate was online now. He checked his profile and saw the little green button under it that indicated he was, indeed, online.

IM or email, that was the question.

Brandon thought it over. There was something, he'd always thought, intrusive about the instant message. He felt it was the cyberspace equivalent of barging into a room and expecting to be paid attention to. Not his style.

He typed a quick email.

*Nate,*

*I'd love to meet you. How about Friday night? Let's do the bar. After the workweek, I'd love nothing better than a Slow, Comfortable Screw. LOL. Actually, I'm a beer guy myself. Seven? Who's Hannah?*

*Just Brandon*

Did his message sound too snarky? He hoped not. He had to be out the door to catch his bus downtown in five minutes. He hit Send.

Brandon gathered up his lunch (leftover lentil soup from last night and a pear) and a few printouts he had brought home with him and started to head out the door.

Nate was online, though. And Brandon *was* curious. Maybe he'd already responded.

*What the hell? There will be another express bus in a bit.* Brandon returned to his computer and checked. Sure enough, there was a message.

*Hey,*

*Is my face red or what? LOL. You probably think I'm insane. Pretty simple explanation, really. I share a town house with my older sister, Hannah. She was standing in the doorway of my room, talking to me when I was writing to you, so I just slipped and said her name instead of my own.*

*Rest assured, I am all man—with more than sufficient proof (wink).*

*And if you think I'm insane? Well, you're right.*

*Still, you've already committed to Friday night. I'll see you at Union at seven.*

*Nate, Nate, Nate, Nate...*

Brandon headed out the door once more. The summer morning was bright. He smiled, not even aware of it.

Friday couldn't get here soon enough.

# Chapter Nine

"So what you want to do is let him down gently," Hannah said.

Nate eyed her. "Really? That makes about a half dozen times you've told me that. Why does it matter to you, anyway? What if I like him?"

The question made Hannah's stomach flutter, because she wasn't sure if she didn't know the answer or that she *did* know the answer and didn't like it. Still, Nate had to agree that the best course of action, after her little online impersonation, was to nip this situation in the bud. "You said it yourself—being with him would make you feel like I pimped you out. And that's just too weird, baby brother. No, there are more gay men in Seattle than you can shake a stick at—or something that rhymes with it—so I think you can pass this one by." Hannah chuckled. "Even if he is adorable."

"I know you're right. I'll meet with him, and I'll make sure it doesn't work out. Lord knows I've been on enough dates that didn't go anywhere that I have the drill firmly imprinted on my brain."

Hannah watched her brother as he pulled clothes from his closet and dresser, flinging them on his king-size bed, considering, and then going back for more.

"I don't know why you're so concerned about your appearance," Hannah said. "Most likely, it'll be one drink and you're out of there. You'll never see him again." And, Hannah thought sadly, *I'll never hear from him again.*

Nate regarded her through suspicious eyes. "Sis? It's me. Nate. You remember? The vain one? It doesn't matter that this isn't going to go anywhere. I still have to look my best, especially since I'm meeting up with a hot gay guy. One never knows who one might meet."

"So, with the gays, it's kind of like a competition?"

Nate shook his head, smirking. "No. But I do believe in leaving them wanting more." He winked and picked up a pair of Howe dark denim jeans. "These will do." He scanned the T-shirts and button-downs on his bed and finally selected a blue collared shirt with white pinstripes. "Good?"

Hannah nodded. The blue of the shirt would bring out the blue in her brother's eyes and contrast with his blond hair. Sometimes, she thought Nate hogged all the looks in their little family. She regarded herself in the mirror over the dresser. She had the same big blue eyes as her brother, but her curly red hair, slight overbite, and heavens-to-Betsy rack caused her to think, as she always had, she had a kind of bizarre little girl/sexy freak thing going on—and the two were very much at odds with each other.

*No wonder Nate got all the men too.*

*Your day will come. And you are* not *unattractive. Not by any stretch.*

"I'll just wear these with some running shoes. Nice and casual. You need to vamoose. I'm going to shower now. I only have about an hour until I have to go."

Hannah rose from the bed, where she had gotten very comfortable, and padded downstairs to her bedroom. There she took out a black jersey top, black tights, and a pair of ballet flats. She wound her hair into a bun on top of her head, holding it in place with a scrunchie, and then hid her red locks under a black woolen cap. She regarded herself in the mirror, giggling. "I look like I'm going to burgle somebody."

The thought wasn't that far off base, since she was planning a covert operation. Who knew if Brandon would ever be a part of her life, their lives? Tonight, he would most likely float out of it for good.

Hannah wanted to see him. She simply could *not* miss out on the opportunity. She also hoped to ensure that Nate did what he was supposed to do—get rid of him and not take him home to bed. Or blow him in the bathroom of the bar. Yes, she had heard stories.

She loved her brother dearly, but the man was a whore, and she knew from personal experience he could sink lower than a snake's belly when it came to sex.

So she would go to Union and have a drink too. She had been to the bar before with Nate and knew the layout. Although it was small, it was also dark, with two-top tables and booths across from its vintage, mirror-backed bar. She figured she could easily conceal herself. And Union was the kind of place people began their evening, rather than ended it, so it was likely to have a decent crowd, making her concealment easier.

*When did you become so deceitful?* She thought and realized quickly: *the moment I posted that ad as Whos2know.*

Her ears perked up as she heard her brother tromping down the stairs. She was glad she had closed her door. He tapped on it now.

"Yes?"

"Okay if I come in?"

One thing about adult siblings sharing a town house—respect for the other's privacy was paramount.

"Actually, I was just getting ready to take a bath, so I'm not decent."

"All right. I just wanted you to tell me if I looked okay."

"Brother, please! I don't need to see you to know you look better than okay." And that, at least, was the truth. He was probably a vision. *Probably? Hah!* "Have fun tonight, and remember..."

"Don't swallow?"

"No."

"Let him down gently. I know, I know."

She listened as Nate made his way down to the main floor, then moved to her window, where she watched her brother, who did look very delicious indeed, don his helmet and climb aboard his orange Vespa scooter. "You little shit," she whispered. She continued to watch as he backed out of the drive and disappeared from sight.

She hurried down the stairs and grabbed her purse where she had left it at the bottom. She hopped in her own car—a sensible, late-model silver-gray Honda Civic—and headed in the direction of Union. She knew that with Nate on his scooter she could get there before him. Only one problem—parking on the Hill on a Friday night was notoriously a challenge.

She might arrive at their destination before her brother, but it would be unlikely she would find parking first, not with Nate on a scooter, which could fit just about anywhere.

Details, details. She sped down to Broadway and Union, eyes on the alert two blocks before the bar for parking spaces.

And luck was with her. Her brother called it Doris Day parking—where one simply pulled up in front of one's destination, no problem. Just as she arrived parallel to the Union, an SUV's backing lights came on. Screeching to a sudden halt, Hannah threw on her turn signal, which almost wasn't enough to prevent the pickup behind her from rear-ending her. The driver honked and sped around her, indicating his rage with speed and an upraised middle finger.

"Sorry!" Hannah mouthed as the pickup sped by, its baseball-capped driver glaring. "Hey, you have to be ruthless if you want a good parking space in this 'hood."

She waited for the SUV to pull out.

*

What Nate loved about his scooter was he could find parking almost anywhere—he could squeeze between two parked cars if necessary. But tonight that luck was not holding. He circled around the blocks adjacent to Union several times before finding a spot.

By the time he approached the bar's discreet black-glass door, he saw that he was already five minutes late. He shrugged. Five minutes late was ten minutes early for Nate.

He pushed open the door, and the thumping bass of nineties dance music rushed out, as if it had been held captive behind plate glass. Nate bobbed his head to "I Saw the Sign" as he waited for his eyes to adjust from the dusky light outside to the dimness of the bar. He scanned the Friday-night crowd, looking for a guy who was also on the lookout for someone, for an expectant look on a very handsome and bearded face.

That would be Brandon.

Although there were several admiring glances cast his way, he saw no one who resembled the picture he had seen of Brandon, nor the image he had imprinted in his mind from their brief encounter at Green Lake. What he *did* spy was fortuitous, though—a booth at the back. Two men were just getting up from it. Nate hurried to claim it.

He sat down, pushing their empty glasses aside, and waited. A server, a black-clad young guy with a shaved head, pierced nose, and a tattoo sleeve that looked brightly colorful even in the dimness of the bar, hurried over with a tray and began wiping the table with a damp cloth as he removed the glasses and bowl of nuts. He made eye contact with Nate, and Nate had to admit, he admired the guy's intense brown eyes. They held the contact for a bit longer than what was normal. Nate thought once he was through with Brandon, he could get this guy's number, not that he didn't already have it, in a sense.

The server grinned, revealing perfect white teeth. Damn, he was a fine specimen. "What can I get you tonight, handsome?"

"You flatterer. How about a Mac and Jack's?" Nate requested one of his favorite local brews.

"Coming right up." The server started away, then stopped. "My name is Coty. I'll be taking care of you tonight." He winked, and Nate thought that neither subtlety nor professionalism was a strong suit for Coty. Still, he enjoyed the attention. "You alone tonight?"

Nate kind of wished he was, but he was honest. "Actually, I'm meeting someone." He glanced down at his watch. "But he's fifteen minutes late."

Coty leaned in, whispering. "I hope he doesn't show."

"Why is that?"

"I'm off at nine."

Nate smiled. "How nice for you."

Coty hurried away, leaving Nate hoping his remark wasn't taken as a dig. He wanted to hedge his bets. He surveyed the bar, checking to see if Brandon had arrived yet and to see if there was anyone he knew there. There wasn't, which made him glad once more that Seattle was a big enough town that one could go out and *not* run into the same crowd over and over.

He slid back and put his feet up on the bench seat across from him, imagining how things would go with Brandon. He visualized the dark-haired guy sitting across from him and imagined how their conversation might play out.

*"So, listen, I have to be honest with you. I'm kind of involved with somebody right now."*

*"But your profile said you were single,"* Brandon said. *"Are you playing games?"*

*"Not at all. I just met this guy, actually, this weekend, and we really hit it off. You know how it goes. I don't know where this might lead, but he checks all the right boxes, you know? I just want to see how stuff might progress before I take things any further with you. Does that make sense? I'm a one-man kind of guy."*

Even Nate had to snicker at that last imaginary statement. A one-man kind of guy? Seriously? Maybe one at a time when he was in a sling...

Brandon would understand and would nod sympathetically. *"I get it. I actually kind of admire you for it. And I have to admit, I'm a little jealous. So if things don't work out with this guy, I hope you'll get in touch."* Brandon, in Nate's mind's eye, smiled, but there was sadness in his eyes.

*Gently*, Hannah had said.

This little reverie was interrupted by Coty, who showed up with his beer and, presumably, with Brandon. "Look what I have for you," Coty said, gripping Brandon's shoulder and shoving him forward. "The beer is six bucks, but we'll have to negotiate over this boy."

Brandon was suddenly in front of him, big as life and smiling. He was just as good-looking as Nate remembered from the brief moment when they passed each other at the lakefront and way better than the picture posted with his profile. Nate's stomach did a somersault.

The server, Coty, faded into the background in more ways than one. He set the beer in front of Nate and moved away. Nate thought the poor guy could probably see it on his face—he had eyes only for Brandon.

And what eyes this Brandon had! He supposed this was what people referred to as hazel, although Nate suddenly had no idea why. What did hazel mean, anyway? But Brandon's eyes, framed by long black lashes, were beautiful. A ring of pale brown, almost amber or gold, surrounded his pupils. The outer area was a pale, warm green, flecked with yellow. Nate felt like he could dive into those eyes. There was something arresting about them. Nate didn't go in much for clichéd sayings, but the old saying about eyes being the window to the soul suddenly made sense. Staring into the warmth of Brandon's eyes in just that instant, Nate felt like he knew Brandon, as though they had met before.

Finally, it was Brandon who broke the moment—and dropped his gaze to the table. "Mind if I sit?"

Nate laughed. "Sorry for staring, but you have the most amazing eyes I've ever seen." Nate didn't usually gush. Most times he was the recipient of the gushing, especially over his own large baby blues. But the words slipped heedlessly from his lips. "Please, sit down, sit down!"

Brandon took a seat across from him. If anything equaled the intensity and sheer pull of Brandon's eyes, it was his smile, which he now revealed. The smile was far from perfect. Brandon's mouth pulled up more on the left than it did on the right, and his front teeth had a small gap. But these things, rather than detracting from his good looks, made him different, unique—and disarmingly sexy.

Nate was a handsome man. He knew this in a very objective way and because he was used to being the focus of attention and flattery. It had always been this way, ever since he had come out in his teens.

But tonight, he suddenly doubted himself, wondering if he was in the same league as Brandon. He couldn't remember a time when he had been more attracted to another man, and, let's face it, he'd been attracted to more than a few.

It wasn't just Brandon's looks that had synapses firing in his brain, had his skin tingling, had his dick rising of its own accord to half-mast and maybe more, but the odd connection he felt with this man. It was as though he had been missing from Nate's life and all of a sudden he realized it, like a puzzle piece falling into place.

Brandon cocked his head, running a hand through his cropped dark hair and making it stand on end. When he spoke again, Nate luxuriated in the deep timbre of the man's voice. "So... I have to ask. What the hell are you thinking about? You look a million miles away, man."

Before he could answer, Coty returned, looking Brandon up and down as a pit bull might eye a T-bone. "What can I get you, sweetie?"

"I'll have what he's having." Grinning and never removing his gaze from Nate's, Brandon nodded across the table.

Coty hurried away, most likely steaming.

Nate could not think of a word to say. Everything that had been in his head, all the planning he and Hannah had done, disappeared like an errant puff of smoke caught on the wind once he had engaged gazes with Brandon.

*Is this what love at first sight feels like? Or is this just a pair of hormones calling to one another? Whatever. Did it matter?* Nate felt a rush of euphoria course through him, as though he had been injected with the most wonderful drug in the world.

Brandon chuckled. "You gonna answer me? You're still a million miles away."

For perhaps the first time in his life, Nate knew no way to respond other than simply blurting out the truth. "I am *not* a million miles away." He picked up Brandon's hand from the table and squeezed it. The resulting skin-to-skin contact was like a jolt of electricity to his heart—and to his groin. "I am so right here. With you."

Brandon looked up as Coty set his beer in front of him. "That's good."

They were silent again. This was as awkward a first date as he had ever had, Nate thought. Is that what this was? A date?

"I'm sorry to be so inept. I'm usually very talkative. My sister can't get me to shut up, says I have no off button." Nate paused, considering whether he should say what was on the tip of his tongue to utter: *I feel this strange and immediate connection to you. It goes beyond attraction. I want to know everything about you. I want to spend the rest of the night with you. And beyond. I want to touch you, to kiss you, to make love to you and not just to fuck. I want everything.*

*I want you.*

He knew if he said those things, Brandon's response would most likely be "Check, please!" So Nate simply said, "You're just so much *more* than your picture." He shook his head, eyeing Brandon. "A picture, I think, doesn't do you justice."

Color rose to Brandon's cheeks, and damn if it didn't make him look even more fetching. "Oh, get out of here," Brandon said softly. "You're the one."

*Am I?* Nate wondered. *The one?*

"Yeah. You look like you just stepped off a runway or a movie set."

Nate laughed.

"I don't even know if I'm in your league."

Nate held up a hand. "Don't. Even. Go there. False modesty is not a pretty sight, not in one so pretty."

Brandon sighed, rubbing his hand over his beard. Even his nervousness was cute. "Okay. So why don't we just talk? Enough with the mutual admiration crap. I can't handle it." Brandon sipped his beer. Nate wanted to lick the foam off his moustache. "So what made you get on OpenHeartOpenMind?"

For a moment, Nate drew a blank and wasn't sure what Brandon was talking about. Then it clicked, and he remembered that was the name of the site where "his" profile was posted. He should have done a little more research before heading out this evening. All he could do was shrug and mumble something about wanting to meet a nice guy. He changed the subject, lest Brandon press him more about a site Nate knew next to nothing about. "So, Brandon, did you realize we've crossed paths before?"

Brandon looked at him, dark eyebrows moving toward each other. "We have? Now that you mention it, I thought you looked familiar, but I just couldn't place from where."

"I run. Green Lake." Nate grinned. "Just last week. I know I cruised you. I'm not sure you cruised me back." Nate allowed himself to laugh, feeling he was now on firmer footing.

Brandon got a faraway look on his face. "Yes! Yes, now I remember. That *was* you. I thought, and I am not being modest here, that you couldn't have been looking at me. Because I knew I wasn't hot enough for you."

"Please! I'm gonna fling this beer in your face." *And then I am going to slowly lick it all off.*

"Sorry. I just don't see myself as such a prize."

"Are you serious?"

Brandon nodded. "I mean, I know I'm not an ogre or anything, but I just don't think I'm all *that*. When I look in the mirror, I see a pretty average-looking guy, pleasant enough, but nothing, as they say, to write home about." He shrugged. "Which is probably why I am heading rapidly toward thirty, still single, and no prospects on the horizon."

Nate thought Brandon was even more appealing for his lack of self-awareness about his looks. A hot guy who didn't know he was hot? That was a rare and beautiful find. Most of the good-looking men Nate had crossed swords with in the past, so to speak, were well aware of their own stud quotient. He eyed Brandon up and down, a pleasure in and of itself, and realized his modesty was not an act. Look at the way he dressed—no tight, muscle-revealing shirt, no faded and crotch-hugging jeans. No, Brandon wore a simple white cotton button-down and a pair of khaki-colored jeans. Nate hadn't yet checked out his feet, but surmised his footwear would be nothing more than some running shoes—Nikes or Asics, maybe.

"And here I thought you were still single because you were picky."

Brandon took a gulp of his beer, then wiped away the foam from his upper lip with the back of his hand. "Well, I am that." He leaned in close. "You read my ad."

Nate's mind went blank. Hannah had shown him the ad, but for the life of him, he could not remember a single word Brandon had said in it. He hoped this little charade was not going to be more difficult than he had imagined. "Yeah..." Nate said, leading.

"Well then, you know that romance is what I'm all about." Brandon's hazel eyes bored into Nate's own blue ones, searching, Nate supposed, for a kindred spirit. What people didn't know about Nate, mainly because of his freewheeling, tomcat lifestyle, was that he was all about romance, too, in every aspect.

"Me too," Nate said and could see he had struck a chord with Brandon. Something lit up in his eyes. "That's not something to admit to these days, not with casual hookups so easy, like..."

"Ordering a pizza," Brandon finished for him, and they both laughed. "I don't order in much at all. I like to cook at home so I know the ingredients, know what I'm putting in my mouth." He raised his eyebrows.

Nate nodded. "I get you." *Oh Lord, maybe Hannah is right, and I should just forget about this dude. He's way too sweet for the likes of me. He probably only has sex when it's "meaningful" or with someone he "cares deeply about."* Nate wasn't sure he knew what that felt like, not anymore. He had been so used to scratching that itch whenever there was the slightest tingle that sex and love for him had become almost polar opposites. Still, as he stared at Brandon across the table, he realized he could change his ways, wanted to change his ways, would change his ways—if only Brandon would allow him.

*Let him down gently*, Hannah spoke in his mind. *No, damn it. I didn't know going in that I was going to fall for the guy.*

"There you go again," Brandon said. "A million miles away." He cocked his head. "Is there someplace else you need to be?"

"Nowhere in the world. I'm sorry. Would you believe me if I said all my thoughts are focused on you?"

"I'd be flattered." Brandon drained his beer. "Getting back to that pizza, I'm kind of hungry. I haven't eaten anything since I had a bowl of pho downtown at lunchtime. Would you wanna extend this to dinner?"

"Would I? Hell, yes. The chance to spend more time with you? Who could say no to that?"

"Really, Nate, the flattery is nice, but stop it. I'm gonna start thinking you're not sincere."

"Oh, I'm sincere all right. How about this for sincere, or at least honest: I know it's way too soon and it's probably wildly inappropriate and definitely juvenile, but would you mind if I kissed you?"

"What? Right here in the bar?"

Nate nodded, grinning. He liked the way the blush rose to Brandon's cheeks, contrasting deliciously with his dark beard. "Right here. Right now." And he stood up, leaned across the table, lifted Brandon's face by his chin, and kissed him. The kiss was sweet, tender, openmouthed, but Nate had the presence of mind to keep his tongue in his own mouth, at least for this first kiss. He noticed that Brandon had not closed his eyes either, which he liked, and that those hazel irises weren't darting about the room, checking to see if anyone was looking. No, Brandon's eyes met Nate's, in almost blurry close-up, and the connection with their eyes was just as powerful as the one with their lips.

When they pulled away, after what seemed like ten minutes, but was probably more like ten seconds, several people in the bar broke into applause, laughing. If you had asked Nate if Brandon could turn any redder a moment ago, he would have said no. But the guy was positively scarlet now, his sheepish grin making Nate want to fly across the table and kiss him again, lick his beard, plant fluttery kisses upon his eyelids.

His hard dick, straining against the denim, urged him to do all those things, but his other head told him he would mortify poor Brandon, so he sat back down, a little breathless. "Let's go eat."

Brandon nodded. When he stood up, Nate could see clearly that his kiss had had the same effect on Brandon as it had on him.

Nate smiled, following.

*

Hannah watched from a corner table. She had blown out the candle on its scarred wooden surface as soon as she sat, making sure she was suitably concealed. All evening, she had been afraid her brother would look over and see her in her spy getup and topple over with sidesplitting laughter. She would be *so* busted. And she had no idea how she would defend herself.

But Nate hadn't seen her. No, his eyes were too busy, first with that sleazy-looking server, who didn't give *her* near the same level of attention as he had given Nate, and then with Brandon.

Her lovely, vulnerable, and sweet Brandon.

Things had not gone at all the way she had planned. What was Nate thinking? Were seductive glances and smiles the way to let someone down gently? And that kiss? There wasn't a whole lot of "letting down" in that lip-lock, for Christ's sake. Hannah thought her brother would swallow the poor boy's face.

She didn't know what had just happened, and she was still reeling from the abrupt change in plans. If Nate and Brandon had been strangers she'd been observing, she would have naturally assumed they were lovers—so intent were their gazes, so familiar was the way they leaned their heads close, like conspirators. And if there had been any doubt in her mind about their familiarity, that kiss would have sealed the deal. It was passion, love, horniness, and a hot-fudge sundae all rolled up into one glorious moment. No wonder the crowd in the bar burst into spontaneous applause. That kiss would have charmed even the congregation of Westboro Baptist Church, it was so damn sweet.

Now Hannah had no idea what to do with her feelings. She pulled off the black wool cap, which was making her too hot, and yanked the scrunchie out, freeing her red curls. She shook her head, and when Coty arrived and pointed to her empty wine glass, a question across his clichéd hipster features, she announced, "Oh, fuck the wine. Bring me a dirty martini, Ketel One if you have it. And make it really dirty." She winked at Coty, who looked at her quizzically, then peered over her shoulder and glanced under the table. "Where did you hide the woman who was just here? The mousy one?"

Hannah laughed. "Just get the damn drink."

Coty hurried away, and Hannah watched the rise and fall of his ass. She pulled out her phone and texted Marilyn: *Fancy a drink?*

Marilyn must have been waiting by the phone because she texted right back: *Where you at?*

*At Union, on the hill. Gay bar and I need some straight company.*

*Who said I was straight?*

*Get out. Are you coming or what?*

*Yeah, yeah. Just as soon as I finish coming, I'll throw some clothes on and get my fat ass down there. Any cute gay guys out?*

*Scads*, Hannah texted back, but did not add—but the two hottest ones just left.

Coty returned, setting not one, but two chilled martini glasses before Hannah. "What's this?"

Coty pointed at the glasses and said slowly, "One plus one makes two."

"But I didn't order two."

"No, you didn't. But the gentleman at the bar decided you might want a second."

Hannah looked over at the bar, where a middle-aged guy wearing a suit with a loose tie around his neck grinned at her. He was cute in an accountant-going-to-seed sort of way, with a little potbelly, thinning blond hair, and wire-rim glasses. He raised a short glass to her. There was something sweet in his smile.

"Now wave back and mouth thank you to the nice man," Coty instructed.

Hannah begrudgingly did so. She turned back to Coty, grumbling, "I thought this was a gay bar."

"Oh, honey, we get all sorts in here." He looked her up and down and raised his eyebrows. "*All* sorts."

Hannah locked eyes with the stranger. *Good God, he sure isn't Brandon. But there's something about his little face. It's got this kind of welcome-home vibe.* Hannah couldn't, in spite of her upset earlier, keep the grin from spreading across her features. *Oh Lord, here he comes.*

The guy had picked up his drink and was moving toward her. In seconds, he was standing before her, and Hannah could see he was probably in his forties and that her assessment that he was cute was confirmed. He was sort of a poor man's Bruce Willis.

"Before you sit down," Hannah said, emboldened by three glasses of wine and several sips of her deliciously chilled martini, "I need to make one statement and ask one question."

"Okay." He eyed her. His voice was husky.

"Statement: I am waiting for a friend. A girl friend. But not a *girlfriend*, if you get my meaning."

"Glad to hear it."

"Question—you married? You might as well be up front about it now. And by married I mean wife, husband, boyfriend, girlfriend, significant other, partner, main squeeze…" Hannah's voice trailed off. "If you're stepping out on a dachshund, now's the time to fess up."

The guy chuckled, sat down, and extended his hand. "Walt Briggs."

Hannah took his hand and gave it a squeeze. "Hannah Tippie."

"You mean tipsy?"

"No. Not yet, anyway. And you haven't responded to my statement or my question, to which I'd like to add another. What brings you to a gay bar?"

Walt put up his hands in defense. "Hey. Patience is a virtue. And I'm hoping you don't have much virtue, so maybe that's a good sign."

Hannah rolled her eyes, but inside, she was tickled. *Oh, don't let him be married. Don't let him be gay.*

"Anyway, I hope your friend stays away for a bit longer so you and I can get better acquainted. I noticed you when you first came in, but when I *really* perked up and took notice is when you took off that hat. Why, oh why, Hannah, would you hide that fiery mane? It's gorgeous. You're gorgeous."

"Thank you." Hannah felt a little quiver of elation go through her. She felt like a woman dying of thirst who had just been given her first sip of water. "And you're being evasive."

"No, I responded to your statement, and now I'll answer your questions. No, I am not married in any sense of the word. I am not significantly othered. Hell, I'm not even dating. Now, have I been married? Yes, to the sweetest woman in the world."

"What did you do to go and ruin it?" Hannah waited for the other shoe to drop, staring.

And Walt's composure faltered a little. He glanced down at the table. "She passed away three years ago. Car accident on Aurora—head-on; at least it was fast."

Hannah put her hands over Walt's. "Oh Jesus, I'm so sorry."

"Hey, it's okay. I will admit freely that I miss Karen every day. But three years is a long time to be alone." Hannah watched as Walt summoned up a smile.

"I hate to tell you, Walt, but this is pretty much a gay joint. Maybe it's not the best choice for getting back out there."

"Which brings us to your last question, the answer to which is a gay coworker. I work in the buying office at Nordstrom downtown. My buy planner is gay. He's a great guy, and I'm not ashamed to say I love him very much. So I go out with him sometimes. We go to dinner, we go to straight bars, we go to gay bars. It's only fair. Kyle, that's his name, met someone tonight, and the two of them went off together, leaving me..." Walt's brow furrowed as Hannah assumed he groped for the right word.

"Sadly alone?"

"No. I was going to say free to talk to the lovely redhead in the corner." He winked.

"You're a flatterer."

"Sorry. I'll stop."

"Don't you dare."

Just then, another voice, one reminiscent of stage, film, and TV star, Brenda Vaccaro, interrupted. "Well, isn't this a cozy scene?"

Hannah looked up to see Marilyn looking down at the two of them, her gaze moving from Hannah to Walt and back again. Hannah was sure she was mistaken, but her friend did not look happy. Like Hannah, she was garbed all in black. Unlike Hannah, she had loaded herself down with lots of heavy silver jewelry and eye makeup she had put on with a roller. If she hadn't looked so put off, Hannah might have asked if she could have her palm read.

"Hi, hon!" Hannah said brightly. "Pull up a chair. This is Walt."

"Hello, Walt." Marilyn smiled sweetly, too sweetly, and took a seat. "Who does a girl have to fuck around here to get a drink?" she bellowed, and Hannah recoiled, feeling heat rise to her face. Her gaze darted around the room at several slack-jawed faces.

Furious, she whispered, "Jesus, Marilyn. The waiter'll be here in a second. Keep your panties on." Hannah regarded Walt out of the corner of her eye. He was looking at Marilyn with undisguised disbelief. Hannah wanted to say, "She's really nice once you get to know her," but thought that would only make things worse. People always said things like that about hateful people.

Coty hurried over to the table. "No fucks necessary," he quipped. "What are you havin'?"

Marilyn eyed him up and down. "You? On a platter? With an apple stuffed in your mouth?" She glanced at Walt and explained, "I like my men quiet."

"I'm afraid, darling, that's not on the menu tonight. How about a Singapore Sling? A Tom Collins? An appletini?"

"Think you have me pegged, do you, handsome?"

"Of course not. What can I get the lady?"

Marilyn consulted the surface of the table, as if an answer was written there. She looked up. "A shot of Jack. With a beer back—make it a PBR." She narrowed her eyes at Coty. "And don't go trying to second guess me again."

Coty hurried off.

Hannah wondered why her friend had bothered to come out tonight. She certainly didn't seem in a good mood. And, now that she had met Walt, Hannah wished her best friend and coworker had stayed home.

Walt looked at the two of them. Then he said, "Listen, I need to get home to Miriam." He stood and squeezed Hannah's shoulder. "She's my Brussels Griffon, and she's probably at the door right now, with her legs crossed and supper on her mind." He yanked off his tie and put it in his pocket. "It was lovely meeting you, Hannah. Perhaps we can get together again sometime soon for another drink? Dinner, maybe?"

Marilyn harrumphed. Hannah didn't know if she had ever heard anyone harrumph before. It was not a pretty sound, on the same level as a fart, albeit not as literary.

Maybe it was for the best that Walt was going.

"I'd like that," she told him. "Here, let me give you my number." Hannah groped around in her bag for a pen and something upon which to write. She ended up writing her phone number on the back of an old Starbucks receipt. She was sure he'd never call, not with the lunatics she had for friends.

Walt pocketed the scrap of paper, leaned down and gave Hannah a quick kiss—on the mouth. Hannah was too stunned to kiss him back. "Later?" He looked into her eyes, and then she was watching him walk away.

"You and your brother—two of a kind."

"What are you talking about?"

"The men. They swarm around you both like flies on shit."

Hannah sighed and took another sip of her martini. "If only that were true. For Nate, sure, but I must have been having a blackout if you've seen men swarming around me. The last time I dated anyone was three years ago, that plumber from Snohomish who wanted to paint my toenails. Ick!" She eyed Marilyn as the waiter served her shot and beer. "What's gotten into you tonight, anyway?"

"Nothin'. Just feeling peppery. Sorry if I prevented girlfriend here from getting something into her."

"Marilyn! It wasn't like that. I hardly know the man, but he did seem nice."

"Will you see him again?"

"*If* he calls. And that's a big if. You know how men are."

"Yeah. Lovely to look at but impossible to hold." Marilyn looked around her. The bar had begun to fill with a different, younger, and more male crowd. "And there are some lovelies here tonight. Check out that one over there." She nodded in the direction of a young guy who was the spitting image of Jake Gyllenhaal—if Jake Gyllenhaal had an addiction to steroids. The dark-haired beauty wore a form-fitting tank top that showed off his grapefruit-sized biceps and failed to conceal the six-pack beneath the thin Spandex.

"Yum-oh!" Marilyn cried. "I'd love to lick every one of those muscles, starting at his shoulders and working my way down to his calves. And then work my way back up." Marilyn smacked her lips. "Isn't he just dreamy?"

"Yeah. Dreamy." Hannah stared at the door through which Walt had exited, thinking about lost opportunities.

# Chapter Ten

Brandon wasn't sure he was doing the right thing at all. He fitted his key into the front door of his apartment with Nate's breath hot on his neck. He had just met the guy, and they had shared a lovely dinner at an intimate little restaurant called Dinette, talking about everything from their childhoods to their favorite foods, to their mutual dislike for sports, to their hopes and dreams for the future. (Brandon longed to write the great American novel, something along the lines of *To Kill a Mockingbird*, and Nate said he had the exact same wish.)

They had laughed. They had flirted. They had played footsie under the table, and Brandon was amazed at how the touch of this guy's foot could give him a boner with all the firmness of steel. They had shared baguette toasts smeared with liver paté and crowned with pickled red pepper, both agreeing that in Dinette's hands, liver became a delicacy worth eating. They had shared plates of *merguez* meatballs and duck-liver confit.

They accompanied all of the rich food with a lovely Willamette Valley pinot noir, which Nate had, after a sip, proclaimed to the waitress, "Dark and fruity. Just like my man, here."

And Brandon felt like they *were* a couple, basking in the waitress's admiring gaze at the pair of them. For the rest of the meal, she referred to them as "you two" and seemed so charmed by them that she brought them a

Valrhona chocolate terrine at the end of the meal, on the house.

"Just because we're so cute?" Nate had kiddingly asked.

"Just because you're good karma—couples in love." The waitress had winked and walked away.

Perhaps it was the wine, the illusion that they were already a couple, the color of Nate's eyes, the firm globes of his ass as he got up to use the men's room, or the openhearted conversation, that caused Brandon to break his own rule and invite Nate back to his apartment in Green Lake. Likely, it was all of these things. Those, and a case of rampant lust and starry-eyed infatuation.

Brandon had no idea it could happen so fast.

Still, as he opened the door and switched on the little lamp he had on the entryway secretary, he had to wonder what he was doing. His whole purpose in placing the ad that had brought them together was to find a man he could date, with whom he could build anticipation, drawing out the attraction, secure in the knowledge that the wait would only make everything more tantalizing, more welcome, more wonderful.

Yet here he was, bringing a guy home after knowing him for only a few hours. Granted, they had emailed back and forth some, and had just shared a very pleasant dinner in which they had gotten to know a lot about the other. But still, it was only a few hours... How was this different from finding a guy for the night on Grindr or Scruff and in the labyrinths of Manhunt?

He thought of that Carole King song, "Will You Love Me Tomorrow?"

Nate followed him into the living room. "Nice place you've got here."

Brandon went to the little speaker unit and located one of his Oscar Peterson albums on his iPhone and set it in the dock. In a moment, the room was filled with that magical piano, playing Gershwin. He smiled at Nate. "I love Oscar Peterson."

"Me too. Come here." And Nate held out his arms.

Brandon froze. No. This wasn't right. This was not the way he wanted things to go. For one, it was too soon, but that was not what was really bothering him.

What was really bothering him was that Nate was gorgeous. Inside and out. Manly yet vulnerable. Strong yet sweet. With a body built for sin and eyes that could make you melt.

He was thirtysomething, and being that beautiful, that age, and that gay meant he was probably pretty damn experienced.

Brandon withered at the thought of his own paltry sexual résumé, with its duo of clumsy couplings. How could he expect to keep up with this perfect stud who stood across from him in his living room?

And then he realized—*You don't have to do anything tonight. It is possible to simply fix some drinks, go out on your balcony, and just talk some more. You can send him home and make a date for another night. Then maybe one more. Then maybe you can think about being intimate.*

Another voice intruded—*But I want to see him naked! I want to lick him from head to toe. I want to feel his tongue halfway down my throat and, and—up my ass. You dirty boy.*

Fortunately, because Brandon suddenly realized he was the one who was now a million miles away, and the silence was getting awkward, Nate broke it. "Hey, buddy, do you think I could have that drink you asked me back here for?"

"God! I'm so sorry. What would you like? I've got some beer in the fridge—Stella Artois I think—and vodka in the freezer. There's orange juice too. Water?"

Nate came over to him and wrapped him in his arms. He kissed him, and the kiss was long and lingering. Brandon felt like he would faint, felt all the thoughts he had prior to the kiss evaporate like a wisp of steam. He pushed himself away from Nate, because he knew that much more of the kiss and he would simply drop to his knees and begin fumbling with the buttons at the fly of Nate's jeans.

*And just what would be wrong with that?*

No. Brandon had to maintain control. He reluctantly disengaged himself from an embrace that felt like coming home and went to the kitchen. "Beer?"

"Sure." Nate made himself comfortable on the couch, opposite the sliding glass doors. "I bet you have a really pretty view during the day."

"Oh, I do—full-on Green Lake. I'm lucky I found this place. I was one of the first in the building. I love getting up in the morning and watching the light come up over the water, the people and their dogs come out. It's always changing."

Brandon had his breath back, and he grabbed two beers from the fridge and popped them open. They hissed as though they were relieved. "Maybe you'd like to have these out on the balcony? It's a nice night."

Nate took his bottle from Brandon, set it on the glass-topped coffee table. "Is that what you want?"

Brandon looked at him shyly. He bit his lower lip. Just let it come. "No."

Nate hooked his fingers in the belt loops of Brandon's jeans and pulled him so their crotches were mashed together. Brandon could feel the other man's excitement, felt his own cock, not only hard, but pulsing in response. Nate kissed him lightly. "What do you want, Brandon?" he whispered, biting Brandon's earlobe. Brandon wondered if his knees were about to go out from under him.

"Everything. I want everything."

"Then let me give you that." Nate took the beer bottle from Brandon's hand and set it next to his own on the coffee table. He pulled away but then grasped Brandon's hand, tugging toward the darkness off the end of the hallway. "This way to the bedroom?"

"Yes." *This is so wrong. This is so right. I should stop. I should wait. I can't.*

Without another word, he followed, letting Nate lead him down to the doorway of his bedroom. At the threshold, Brandon said, voice hoarse with need, with want, "I have to tell you something."

"What? You're poz? We'll deal with it. There's someone else?" Nate shook his head. "Don't like that, but we'll deal with that too, later."

Brandon slumped against Nate's chest. "Nothing like those things." Brandon took a deep breath. "I'm practically a virgin," he blurted out, feeling familiar heat rise to his face.

Nate chuckled, but there was nothing unkind about it. "You're kidding, right? A guy who looks like you? You could have anyone you wanted."

"That's just it. I didn't want anyone—not until now. Not until it was right." Brandon felt a weird mixture of lust, despair, hope, and imminent tears. No! "Are *you*... right?"

Nate pulled him into the dark room so they were sitting on the bed.

Brandon said, "Please. I wanted to take things slow. I didn't want things to go this fast." He smiled, realizing the redundancy of what he had just said. But what the hell, he was nervous. "But I do—so much—want things to go this fast. Faster." He undid the top button of Nate's jeans. "Are you right?" he repeated.

"Yes. I think I am."

"Will you understand if I'm not good at this? Will you be patient?"

Nate chuckled again, shucking off his jeans so when he sat on the bed he was wearing only his boxers and T-shirt. "Look, sweetie, people give too much credence to experience. Sex is natural. It's kind of in our DNA to know what to do. We pick up a few moves here and there, but, really, when it comes right down to it, if you just go with what feels right, you're gonna be good. Push your mind out of the way; let your body take over. I know *you'll* be good. All you need to remember are three things: relax your lips, watch your teeth, and go slow." He drew out the last word. "Now take off your clothes."

Their eyes met in the shadows, and Brandon stood, tentative, and began to undress. He didn't remove his gaze from Nate's stare the whole time he stripped with trembling hands. He almost stumbled and fell as he struggled out of his jeans.

But at last he was naked.

Nate sat on the bed, saying nothing, and Brandon wondered if he was disappointed. But all it took to replace that fear was one look at his face. Nate's handsome features revealed nothing but delight and anticipation. Nate quickly shucked what clothes he had left on and stood. "Lie down on your back."

Brandon complied, suddenly feeling like this was not his third time with a man, but his first. He hoped his trembling limbs would not be obvious to Nate, hoped his inexperience wouldn't make the whole enterprise they were about to engage in a disaster.

Nate sat next to him on the bed. Brandon allowed himself a quick glance at the cock rising up from between Nate's thighs and thought of the phrase "purple-helmeted warrior" he had once read somewhere. The cock oozed a drop of precome at its tip, which Brandon had an almost irresistible urge to rise up and lick away. His own cock twitched with the thought.

Nate spoke softly. "I just want you to relax. I want you to leave tonight entirely in my hands. Trust me to ensure you have a very good time." Nate stood. "You have any candles?"

"What?" Brandon whispered. "You gonna drip hot wax on me?"

Nate chuckled. "No, silly. I'd just like to make things a bit more *romantic*. Set the mood."

Brandon's mind went blank. He wasn't big on candles. He didn't take bubble baths by the light of them, but he did remember the sterling silver candlesticks that had belonged to his mom on his dining room table. There were two white taper candles, never lit, in them. "On the table—out there," Brandon mumbled.

"I'll go get them."

In moments, Nate returned bearing the two candles aloft, their flickering light illuminating his face from below. Brandon couldn't decide if he looked demonic or angelic; a bit of both, he supposed.

Nate set the candles atop the dresser and returned to the bed. "Close your eyes."

"What?"

"Close your eyes. Put yourself in my hands."

Brandon closed his eyes, thinking, absurdly, *This is where he pulls out the hunting knife.* But all Nate pulled out were two warm and strong hands. He gripped the sides of Brandon's face and leaned in close to plant a feathery kiss on his lips. His hands traced their way down Brandon's body, lingering over his nipples, twisting them to that ultra-thin line between pleasure and pain. Brandon gasped. Nate moved on, brushing his fingers over the treasure trail that coursed over Brandon's stomach. He ignored Brandon's cock and moved on to his thighs, which he massaged gently, working downward to his feet. He took a couple of Brandon's toes in his mouth and sucked. Brandon cried out, "That tickles!"

Nate pulled away. "Does this?" And he engulfed Brandon's cock with his mouth, swirling his tongue around the shaft, burying his nose in Brandon's pubes. His dick was engulfed in heat and wet; his hips bucked of their own accord.

It was too much. It had been too long. Brandon knew it was too fast, hated that it was too fast, but the pulses were already coursing through him like waves of electricity. "Oh fuck! I'm so sorry, but I'm gonna come!"

Nate did not remove his mouth, but simply held on to Brandon's bucking thighs and stomach as he pumped his seed down Nate's throat. Nate's eloquent response? "Mmmmm."

Nate stayed with him until his orgasm ebbed away, his dick pulsing. He then moved up to Brandon's face. "Taste yourself." He leaned in for a deep kiss, and Brandon could taste the seawater tang of his own semen on Nate's tongue and lips, and it got him hard all over again.

He whispered, "I'm sorry I shot so quick."

"Sorry? What for? I can't imagine a nicer compliment," Nate whispered. "Or a tastier one." He ran his fingers through the hair on Brandon's chest, finally resting his head where his fingers had lit. He said softly, "Besides, we have all night, and I have a feeling..." He squeezed Brandon's cock, causing him to shudder. "I have a feeling that you, sir, are good for more than just one money shot." He laughed.

"I think that's a bet you have a good chance of winning," Brandon said. "Come here and kiss me again."

The night continued, with the warm, briny smell of the lake coming in through Brandon's open bedroom windows, chilling them and spurring them on to more friction, the exchange of more bodily heat.

Nate did win the bet. And so did Brandon—three times. When morning's gray light began to infuse the room, both of them had yet to sleep.

Now, as they watched the passage of the day creep into the room, they lay in one another's arms, spent and contented.

"Next time—you'll fuck me?" Nate whispered.

Brandon nodded. They had done so much the night before and into the dawn, but he wanted to hold something back for Nate, something special. And for Brandon, that something was fucking. There were times, especially when Brandon was eating Nate's hot, sweet, clean ass that he wanted to simply rise up and plow his way inside Nate, but he was somehow able to control himself, knowing that to leave something unexplored would make it all the sweeter when the moment did come.

"I will. And maybe you'll do the same for me."

Nate pushed Brandon over on his side, Brandon supposed, so he could regard his ass. "Usually, I bottom, but for this, I think I could be persuaded to be versatile." Nate's voice was husky with desire, and part of Brandon wanted to edge his ass closer to Nate's cock, but knew that a movement of even an inch could ruin his plans for delayed gratification. "Wait a minute. You said, 'next time.' That means there will be a next time, right? And by that, you mean not in just the next ten minutes?"

Nate ruffled Brandon's hair. "Silly boy. Of course there will be a next time. I hope there will be many next times—over weeks, months, hell, maybe even years. You need to take some confidence in yourself." Nate looked into his eyes. "You're wonderful."

"Ah, get out."

Brandon relaxed, his head on the pillow, mumbling something about making breakfast for the two of them, but the warmth of Nate's body next to his, the sated aura surrounding him, and the cool lake breeze blowing in the window all conspired together to make this bedroom a kind of heaven, a place Brandon never wanted to leave. He snuggled in closer, if that was possible, to Nate.

He drifted off.

# Chapter Eleven

Hannah awakened the next morning feeling as though she had a little man behind her eyes, jabbing away with an ice pick. His kinfolk worked farther south, making her stomach roil with nausea. She groaned, rolling over in bed to stare out the window at the completely and, incongruously, sunny day. "Lord," she whispered, forcing herself out of bed to pull the blinds shut more tightly.

Why had she drunk all those dirty martinis? So many that she lost count! Damn that Marilyn. She was a bad influence.

The two of them had had a couple more at Union, then moved on to R Place, and finally ended up as one of the only pairs of women in the leathery confines of the Cuff. At the moment, Hannah remembered little of the night before, beyond an embarrassing upchuck on Pine Street and watching two guys eat each other's faces late at night in the Cuff. They had made Hannah think of Hannibal Lecter.

And of course she remembered Walt, the sweet touch to the beginning of what otherwise had been a pretty shitty evening.

Would he ever call her?

She knew the answer would be an emphatic "no" if he could have seen her and Marilyn throughout the remainder of their long, drunken night. Hannah shivered with remorse. They were no better than a couple of misguided schoolgirls.

While she was up and out of bed (a place she wondered if she'd really be able to leave at all today, in spite of the summer sun outside), she couldn't resist doing something that was eating at her. She pulled her robe on and opened her bedroom door, listening.

The town house was still. How she longed to hear the sound of Nate's footfalls above her or strains of music from his room. She wanted to smell coffee brewing downstairs.

But the house, as she had known in her heart, was empty.

She crept up the stairs to the master suite Nate occupied and pushed open the door.

His bed was neatly made. She wandered inside, glancing down at his desk and his laptop, shut. His en suite bath was as orderly as his bedroom. She touched the sink and the tumbled marble of the shower enclosure. Her fingers came away dry.

*Damn him.* She hurried back downstairs to her own bedroom, threw off her robe, and flung herself back on the bed. *He was supposed to let Brandon down gently. He wasn't supposed to spend the night with him.*

Hannah told herself she didn't know that Nate had actually spent the night with Brandon. They could have parted after leaving Union together and gone their separate ways. Nate could have hooked up with anyone after that.

But somehow, in her heart of hearts, she knew that wasn't true. She had seen the way they looked at each other, witnessed the connection their eyes and smiles had made. It wasn't logical that there could have been any other outcome than spending the night together.

*Why do you care? What makes the difference*? And Hannah didn't know how to answer herself. She knew only what her body told her—that thinking of Nate and Brandon in bed together made her feel sicker than she already was from over-imbibing the night before. Her head told her the response had no logic to it and certainly not a lick of sense.

*But we feel what we feel.*

Hannah tried to go back to sleep, tossing and turning for another good hour on sheets damp with sweat. At around ten, she got up and threw on a pair of shorts and a T-shirt and padded downstairs. She turned the Keurig on and set a coffee mug beneath its spout. She hunted around for a K-cup that would deliver her the darkest, strongest coffee roast. The acid might not do much for her stomach, but at least it would help clear some of the fog in her head.

While she waited for her coffee, she sat at the dining room table and opened up her laptop with the intention of checking her email, but instead found herself rapidly typing into her browser bar the URL for OpenHeartOpenMind. She logged in and saw she had email from Brandon.

Maybe they hadn't spent the night together after all!

So she almost screamed when she heard the bee-like whine of Nate's scooter pulling up out front. She slammed shut her laptop and moved quickly to the kitchen counter to grab her coffee. She stiffened, as though she had been masturbating or something, when she heard Nate's key in the lock.

Pretending to be nonchalant, she leaned against the kitchen counter, sipping her black coffee and eyeing her brother as he came up the stairs from the front door. In spite of his wind-disheveled hair and wrinkled clothes, he still looked gorgeous, his skin glowing and ruddy from the wind.

"Hey, Sis," he said.

"Good morning!" Hannah chirped, trying to sound awake, trying to sound alive. "Nice night?"

Nate stood facing her, jiggling his keys in one hand. "Oh my God. The best." He grinned and winked.

Hannah's stomach did a flip-flop. She set her coffee down. "Anyone I know?" She would play out the game of ignorance, pretending she hadn't witnessed her brother and Brandon canoodling at the bar the night before. As far as Nate knew, his sister was under the impression Nate had let Brandon down gently.

Nate wagged a finger at her. "You know I don't kiss and tell. I'm beat. I didn't get much sleep. I'll see you when I get up later this afternoon."

And with that, he was gone.

And then he was back. "And you, Sis, need to go back to bed. You look like hell."

He headed back up the stairs.

"Thank you!" Hannah called after him.

It was for the best. He was gone. Her skin was probably a lovely shade of Wicked-Witch-of-the-West green, and that sweat at her hairline would never, under any circumstances, be considered "dewy."

She plopped back down at the table, after grabbing a Franz chocolate-covered donut from a box on the counter. She bit into it as she opened her laptop and her OpenHeartOpenMind email.

There it was, staring her in the face. A message from Brandon, written within the last hour.

*My Sweet,*

*You just walked out the door, leaving the scent of come and sweat trailing after you. I don't think any high-priced designer scent from Paris could smell better.*

*I miss you already. I wish you had stayed for breakfast, stayed to shower (so I could have soaped every inch of your sexy body), stayed another night.*

*Another. And another.*

*Oh, Nate, please don't let this scare you away—but I have fallen for you big time.*

*I can't wait to see you again.*

*Kisses,*

*Brandon*

"That did it." Hannah stood and hurried to the powder room off the kitchen and threw up.

When she returned, her hands were shaking and her skin felt cold and clammy. *Oh Hannah, for heaven's sake, will you please get over yourself? This is not about you. Brandon is not about you. Delete this account.*

But how could she delete the account? Brandon was still writing to it. What would he think if "Nate" was suddenly gone from the site?

Feeling exhausted, nauseous, and with a headache from hell, Hannah hit reply.

*Brandon,*

*You do scare me, buddy. I thought you wanted to take things slow. Get a grip, okay? Let's just see where life takes us.*

*Best regards,*

*Nate*

Hannah paused, finger hovering over the mouse. *Should I do this?* She knew the message was cold, heartless, knew the effect it would have. She pictured Brandon's sweet face, smiling in anticipation, falling as he read the harsh words on his screen. She could empathize.

She didn't click on Send. Instead, her finger moved to the backspace key, and she erased what she'd written and tried again.

*Honey Crisp,*

*You were wonderful. I can't wait to see you again, to get to know you better, to explore all that life has to offer—with you.*

*Last night was the beginning of something magical, wasn't it? When you were deep inside me, my legs up on your shoulders and your sexy eyes boring into mine, I had one thought only—I could love this man.*

*Your Nate*

Was it too much? It was certainly mushy—not to mention explicit—and Hannah was sure it would only advance what she guessed was a budding love affair. Still, she knew her brother and knew how budding affairs usually got nipped by week three, at the latest.

*Why encourage it? Because you're his sister and you love him. Because the good part of you, the one that isn't stupidly and insanely jealous, knows it's the right thing to do.*

She hit Send. Shutting the laptop, Hannah felt proud of herself for a moment, knowing she had just done a very selfless thing.

Hadn't she?

\*

Brandon, in spite of being tired from the lack of sleep, was jazzed. So, instead of his usual three-mile lap around Green Lake, he did two laps, six miles. The whole time, it felt like his feet were buoyed up by air. He felt as though he could run forever. The endorphins coursing through him, his easy respiration, the way his body, heart, and mind worked in perfect unity, made the run a pleasure rather than a chore.

But the best part? The part that made it easy? The whole time, he thought about Nate.

What had happened.

What was to come.

About tonight, when they would have their second date, or first, depending on how you looked at last night. Brandon shrugged and wiped sweat from his brow. Last night would always be their first date to him. It would be first in a lot of ways. Brandon wondered if it was happy or sad that, at almost thirty, this was the first time he had felt this euphoria, this inability to stop thinking about another person.

Tonight, Nate said he would take him to his favorite Vietnamese spot, a little restaurant on Nineteenth called Lotus. "I want to share their amazing food with you," he had said, kissing him at the front door. "I want to share everything with you."

Brandon finished his run, went home, showered, and finally felt his excitement—no—jubilation, ebb enough so that he thought he could sleep. He was heading into the bedroom when he decided to check, real quick, to see if Nate had replied to his message from earlier that morning.

Brandon hoped it hadn't been too much. He prayed it wasn't too little. He hoped it was just right.

He opened OpenHeartOpenMind.

He reread the brief message. At first glance, he was elated. The guy had said he loved him! Or at least said he could! But then he read it again, wanting to savor it, but feeling a bit disoriented. His eyebrows furrowed in confusion.

That one line—about Brandon being inside him, legs up on shoulders—what the hell was that about? The one thing they hadn't done the night before was fuck, and yet here was Nate, talking as though they had.

In all the sweaty, frantic couplings that had happened in the last twelve or so hours, *had* Brandon slipped inside him and forgotten?

He laughed. No, that was *not* possible. Even if he had been drunk out of his mind—and he was most assuredly not—he knew he would remember being inside Nate. My God, it was something he had looked forward to with all of his heart. It was something he thought might happen tonight.

Was it a fantasy? Did he just not get what Nate was trying to say?

That had to be it. Brandon rubbed his fisted hands against his burning eyes. The wine, the beer, the sex, the lack of sleep—all of these things had finally caught up to him, demanding their due. He told himself that perhaps it was only his fatigue causing him to be so puzzled by Nate's cryptic turn of phrase.

He would ask him about it tonight. It would be easier than typing out yet another message to him. What good were these messages, when he could look into Nate's blue eyes as he communicated with him?

He figured he should take down his OpenHeartOpenMind account anyway. He had found what he wanted.

He stripped off his running clothes and slid into his bed, naked. The smell of Nate still clung to the sheets, and he pulled the pillow where Nate's head had lain toward him so he could inhale a big lungful of the man's essence. There still lay on the linen a strand of golden hair, and Brandon brought it to his mouth to taste it.

He could ask Nate about what he had said over dinner. After dinner, Brandon could make what he said come true.

With thoughts like these on his mind, and with half a hard-on, Brandon turned over and fell asleep.

# Chapter Twelve

Hannah had invited Marilyn over to watch a movie. The two of them had *Imitation of Life* all queued up in the DVD player, but had yet to switch it on. The movie was one of Hannah's favorites, and the final, climactic scene, where Susan Kohner runs after her spurned mother's funeral carriage, never failed to elicit buckets of tears from her. Tonight, she knew, would be even worse, wrung out as she was from the partying she had done the night before.

"Oy. I am not as young as I used to be." Hannah's head still pounded. Even though it was a dull thud, it still hurt.

"What do you mean?" Marilyn pulled the big bowl of popcorn between them closer to her and dug her hand in it. She was dressed for comfort tonight, in a pair of old sweatpants and a University of Washington sweatshirt. She wore no makeup, and her dark hair hung lifeless about her face. In spite of her athletic apparel, she looked to be about sixty, when Hannah knew she was at least twenty years younger than that.

"Oh, come on, sweetie. You know exactly what I mean. There used to be a time when I could go out clubbing like we did last night, and by this time next day, after a big greasy cheeseburger for lunch, I would be feeling pretty much okay. But I feel like I've gone ten rounds with a prizefighter."

"Oooh...wouldn't that be nice?" Marilyn crossed and uncrossed her legs, snorting.

"Ten rounds in the ring. Ten rounds that ended with me getting a hard left hook to my face. Down for the count." Hannah popped a kernel into her mouth. "Get your mind out of the gutter—for once." She wasn't hungry. The idea for the snack was Marilyn's. Marilyn also had the idea for a nice tall vodka and cranberry, which rested now on a coaster in front of her. The thought of more alcohol made Hannah want to puke. She was sticking with a Diet Coke, thank you very much. She needed the hydration, and the caffeine would keep her awake long enough to get to the scene where she could bawl like a baby.

Nate padded down the stairs, and Hannah didn't miss how Marilyn sat up, more alert, sucking in her gut a bit and fluttering her hands about her hair, patting it. She smiled prettily. "Why, Nate! Aren't you just a sight for sore eyes!" Marilyn cried. "Come over here and give Mama a big kiss."

Hannah rolled her eyes and then made a *tsk* sound as Marilyn forced what was obviously intended to be a peck on the cheek into a full-on kiss on the lips. Nate pulled away, dabbing at his lips with the back of his hand. "You seem to have survived last night better than my sister here."

"Ah—I'm made of stronger stuff. Got a hot date tonight?"

"Why, yes, in fact, I do. Dinner at Lotus, and then we'll see where the night takes us."

"Yeah, right. We'll see." Marilyn sneered. "You and I both know where the night will take you—straight to bed." Marilyn barked out a gruff laugh that ended in a fit of coughing.

"Doesn't the guy need some rest? Weren't you two up all night last night?" Hannah asked. "Lord, to be young."

Nate shrugged. "I think when it comes down to a choice between some Nate lovin' and sleep, the former will always win." He winked at Marilyn, who was in the process of sucking down about half her cocktail. She nodded at him, an ally, over the rim of her glass.

"Do I look okay?" He turned in front of his sister.

"Passable." Hannah pointed the remote at the entertainment unit. Marilyn put a hand over Hannah's to stop her.

"Passable? The man looks like he stepped off the pages of *GQ*."

"I guess he does look nice," Hannah said softly. And he did. Nate wore a pair of ecru linen pants, topped with a chocolate-brown cotton V-neck. A pair of sandals adorned his feet. There was not a hair out of place, and his skin, the pores so tiny they might as well have been invisible, was radiant. In spite of the simplicity of the outfit, Nate did look, well, beautiful, and she agreed with her friend's statement.

Why couldn't she let Nate know that she saw what Marilyn did? Perhaps it was because she would be sitting here on the couch with Marilyn tonight, watching an old Douglas Sirk weeper while her brother was off getting laid. Far too often, Hannah thought, a similar scenario had played itself out.

Why was it never the other way around? Why couldn't Nate stay home for once, while *she* was out, riding some poor man like a jockey on a racehorse? Hannah hit the buttons that would bring the DVD and TV to life.

"Don't wait up for me," Nate called out as he exited.

"Like I would!" Hannah yelled after him, but he had already closed the door.

"You ready for this movie?"

"In a minute. Jesus, what's your rush? You seem agitated."

"I'm still a little hung over." Hannah took a gulp of her Coke.

"So is he going out with anyone special?"

"How should I know?" Hannah snapped. "They're all special—for about five minutes." Hannah hadn't told Marilyn anything about her spying the night before, nor had she mentioned she had kept their online profile alive and was continuing to communicate, via OpenHeartOpenMind's email system, with Brandon. In fact, she had shot him a message just a little while ago, saying she, or rather Nate, was "over the moon" with anticipation about their dinner date that night. "Can we watch the movie now?"

"Sure thing, hon."

\*

Nate had arrived at Lotus early, just so he could watch Brandon as he walked down Nineteenth. He had ordered a beer and had taken one of the tables in front of the bank of windows that made up the front of the restaurant.

Darkness came late to Seattle in summer, so outside, even though it was going on seven, the sky was still a brilliant blue and the street was as bright as midday. Across the street was Miss Amy's, one of the few places in the Pacific Northwest that Nate knew of that served good southern cooking, real down-home soul food—fried chicken, catfish, greens, macaroni and cheese. Maybe he and Brandon could go there next, share a slice of their amazing bourbon brown-sugar cake.

He liked thinking about a future with Brandon; the pieces just seemed to fit.

He moved his gaze from the façade of Miss Amy's and saw Brandon. His heart gave a little skip—for two reasons. One, because, in the short time they were apart, he had forgotten exactly how delicious the man was, with his dark, wavy hair, beard, hazel eyes, and beefy build. He looked like someone who could not only pound you until you screamed, but someone with whom you could cuddle up with afterward, a big, furry man blanket. Nate wondered where Brandon had been hiding all his life.

The second reason his heart experienced a little jolt was because Brandon was not, as Nate expected, alone.

Walking alongside him was a blonde woman. She had a straight shoulder-length bob and was laughing at something Brandon had said, touching his shoulder affectionately.

Who could this be? Brandon's best gal pal? And what kind of message did it send if Brandon was bringing a chaperone?

Nate felt mildly perturbed. He had been looking forward to this evening as a bit of continuity—refining and extending the intimacy and magic of the night before. A third party, no matter how charming and nice, would definitely be an impediment.

And what of later, after dinner? Would Nate's fantasies about another night with Brandon come true? Or would he beg off, saying he had to see his girlfriend here safely home?

He could ponder these questions no longer. They were coming into the restaurant. Nate saw that the woman was older than he first thought—her slight frame and flaxen hair belied her years, which Nate would guess, now that she was closer, numbered in the mid to upper forties.

Brandon's dark eyes met Nate's, and for a moment, he forgot all about the woman with him. Hell, he forgot all about the waitress serving him, the other diners, the cooking staff behind the glass wall at the rear of the little restaurant. What was it about his eyes that got him so riled, that could transport him? Nate stood, and Brandon, without a hint of self-consciousness, hurried over to him, hugged him, and gave him the gift of a soft kiss on the lips.

Nate sat down again—because he needed to. He took a long swallow of his beer for the same reason. The man *sent* him. There was no other word for it.

Brandon took the woman with him by the arm and edged her nearer the table. "Nate Tippie, I'd like you to meet my mother, Nancy Wylde."

The woman smiled. As far as coloring went, she looked nothing like Brandon, yet he could see that her smile, her nose, and the thick dark eyebrows that contrasted with her blonde hair were much like Brandon. Her smile was honest and forthright and maybe, Nate wondered, a little apologetic?

"Pleased to meet you. Brandon's been talking about you since he picked me up tonight." Nancy sighed. "I swear, if I took the word, 'Nate,' out of his vocabulary, poor Brandon would have nothing to say." She laughed, and Brandon reddened—charmingly.

They shook hands, and Nancy sat at the table, after Brandon had pulled out a chair for her. "Brandon has been telling me—*ad infinitum*—all about you on the way over here. He's really quite smitten." She giggled again, and the laugh was that of a young girl's. Nate was charmed.

"Nancy!" Brandon scolded, sitting down next to his mother. "Can we talk about something else?" Again their eyes met, and Brandon gave Nate a shy smile, one just for him. Nate would have to concede that Nancy's powers of observation were pretty spot-on. He knew Brandon was smitten because Nate felt exactly the same.

"We sure can, sweetie, but Mama needs to powder her nose. I'll be right back."

They waited for her to leave. Brandon reached across the table and squeezed Nate's hand. "I hope you don't mind. She called just as I was leaving. A lot of times I have supper with her on the weekends and, well..."

"You couldn't break with tradition?" Nate wondered if this was a red flag.

"No, no. I planned on just saying I had a dinner date with you. But then she told me the news—she lost her job on Friday. They laid her off from the library where she works, has worked for the past fifteen years. She's kind of devastated. She didn't want to horn in, but I insisted. I didn't want her sitting all by herself tonight."

Nate was touched. "You're a good son. I don't mind at all. She seems charming."

"Well, she has her moments. I'm glad you're okay with it." He slid his foot up Nate's calf. "We came in her car, so I'm hoping you'll be able to give me a lift home after we eat." He winked. "Do you get me?"

"Subtle as a sledgehammer, my Brandon." Nate chuckled. Warmth and a kind of amorous electricity surged through him. "I'll give you a lift." He wiggled his eyebrows.

"I just bet you will. Maybe you can stare into my eyes when your legs are on my shoulders?" Brandon laughed.

*Wow*. Nate was surprised at the boy—wasn't he talking about being nearly a virgin just hours ago? This was certainly a forward side of him! Where was it coming from?

"I think that could be arranged."

Brandon took on a more serious mien. "My mom's coming back. Should we get some stuff ordered? I love the woman, but the sooner we can get dinner out of the way, the sooner we can get to dessert."

"What are you boys whispering about? You look like conspirators." Nancy sat back down at the table. "I want that." She pointed at Nate's beer.

"We'll get you one, Mom."

"And some appetizers," Nate chimed in.

"So what were you talking about?"

Brandon replied, "Just the Ferris wheel downtown on the waterfront. Nate has never been. I was telling him I'd like to treat him to a ride—later." Brandon's gaze met Nate's, and Nate could clearly see the mischief there.

"Well, I don't know if I'd be up for that. You know how heights scare me. But you boys go and have a good time. Brandon here has always loved to ride."

"I'm counting on it." Nate grinned. Their waitress showed up, and Nate ordered a round of appetizers for the table: oysters, lettuce cups, and an imperial roll.

Nate turned to Nancy. "So, Brandon has told me a little bit about you. So sorry to hear about the layoff, but glad to hear you like books. What's your favorite genre?"

"I read a lot of biographies and memoirs."

"Nancy. Tell him the truth."

"Okay, my guilty pleasure is romance." She glanced over at her son. "Gay romance. It gives me hope for Brandon here."

Nate slid back in his chair and took a sip of beer. "Ever hear of BF Mann?"

*

Like gentlemen, they both walked Nancy back to her car, parked on Aloha. Brandon hugged his mother and stepped aside so Nate could do the same. All in all, Brandon was happy the dinner had gone so well. Brandon had simply sat back and watched as his mother and Nate got caught up in a lively exchange about, of all topics, gay romance novels. Nate had mentioned some of his favorites—Amy Lane, ZA Maxfield, Ally Blue, AJ Llewellyn, and BG Thomas—and Nancy had read them all, adding in how much she liked GA Hauser and BF Mann.

"What do you think of Mann?" Nate had asked.

"I love that her stories are all set right here in Seattle. They'd be good no matter where you were from or where she set them, but all the familiar places add a dimension of reality for me that I like. I can't wait until she comes out with the new one. What's it called?"

"*Like Father, Like Son*," Nate had shot back. "It's about the detective father and son team competing for the same man, although they don't know it, after the son breaks up with his partner. And, of course, there's a shape-shifter loose in Magnolia." Nate chuckled.

"I will have to preorder it."

Now, as she slid into her car, Brandon leaned in and said, "I'll call you in the morning. Maybe we can do lunch tomorrow?"

Nancy put her hand on his. "Honey, I appreciate that you're worried about me. But I'm a big girl, so don't. I'll find another job." She smiled at him. Looking directly at Nate, she said, "You might want to sleep in in the morning." Her gaze went back to her son. "Don't worry about your old mother. We'll see each other soon."

Brandon watched her drive off. He turned back to Nate, who, even in the dusky light, suddenly looked pale. His skin appeared damp, clammy, even though Brandon would estimate the temperature being only in the seventies. Brandon was shocked at the sudden transformation.

"Are you okay?"

Nate swallowed. "I don't know. I don't feel so good."

"Really? When did this come on?"

"Just now. Like that." Nate snapped his fingers. "Oh Lord, my stomach is churning."

Brandon put a hand on his shoulder. "We should get you home." They continued down the street and stopped at Nate's orange Vespa. Brandon eyed it warily, especially since Nate had gone suddenly and uncharacteristically quiet during the short walk. Brandon was just about to ask him if he felt well enough to drive the thing, when Nate hurried away. They were near the mouth of an alley, and it was there that Nate disappeared.

Brandon, wincing, listened as Nate threw up. He closed his eyes. *Poor guy.* Nate had been the only one who had chicken, in that noodle dish he had ordered. Brandon had contracted food poisoning once and recognized the signs: the sudden onset, the queasiness, the vomiting. He knew it would most likely pass within a day, but still, he knew Nate had a rough several hours ahead of him.

Nate emerged from the alley looking paler than before, shaken. "I'm so sorry," he said. "What a great date I am, huh?" He laughed weakly. "Bet you just can't wait to kiss me."

Brandon moved in close and put his hands on Nate's shoulders. He could smell acid bile on Nate's breath, but he didn't step back and worked hard not to show he even smelled it. "Hey, don't you dare even think that way."

"But I'm sure you were all set for a hot night."

Brandon shrugged. "Yeah, so sue me. But that doesn't change the fact that I am just happy to be with you. Look, I'm sorry that you're sick, but we can do one of two things. First, I call you a cab and send you home in it, so you can take care of yourself in your own bed. I know sometimes when I've felt rotten, all I want is to be alone. Or second, again, I can call a cab, and we'll take it to my place. If you let me, I'll take care of you." Brandon smiled, hoping Nate wouldn't perceive his offer as too forward.

"You'd do that?" Nate eyed him.

"Of course I would. What? Did you think I was just in it for the sex?"

"Well, yeah. Isn't everyone?"

Brandon shook his head. "I am in it for the sex, but for a whole lot more too. I'm a good nurse, and I have an excellent bedside manner."

"I just bet you do." Nate, in spite of his ashen pallor, gave Brandon a smile.

"So, what'll it be? Door One or Door Two?"

"If you don't mind, I'd love to have someone take care of me."

"I was hoping you'd say that."

"Are you sure you don't want to just take the scooter?"

"Not with the way you're looking. Besides, I have no idea how to drive one of those things. We'll splurge on a cab." Brandon pulled his phone from his pocket with one hand. With the other, he guided Nate to lean against a parked car.

"Yes, hello, we need a cab."

*

Brandon got Nate settled in bed. He made sure the window was open wide so it would let in the cool night breeze. He covered Nate with a sheet and light quilt and made him a cup of chamomile tea. Handing it to him, Brandon said, "This will help settle your stomach."

Nate sipped at it, eyeing Brandon over the rim of the mug. "You're too good to be true. My mother always used to say, 'If it sounds too good to be true, it probably is.' So, what's your story, Mr. Wylde? What's your secret? Drug user? Jealous ex in the wings? On the down low? Can't commit? Believe me, I've heard 'em all. And I am just waiting for the other shoe to drop because, honey, I have learned no one is perfect." Nate set his tea down on the nightstand.

Brandon sat on the bed beside him, then brushed a stray lock of blond hair off Nate's forehead. "Do I really have to tell you about the bodies? And where they're buried? And that stint as a hustler? Do you really want to hear about all the tricks I took on and the pimp who beat me? Huh? Can't we just pretend I'm this nice, normal guy who likes nothing better than getting outside to run, or staying in to watch a movie or read a good book?" Brandon swung his legs off the floor so he could lie next to Nate, whose stomach was gurgling. He got up and put the bathroom wastebasket next to the bed, then returned to lying next to Nate. "Maybe my secret is I'm just a bore, an average guy who goes to work, comes home, and does what dozens of other people do every day."

Nate reached over and touched Brandon's beard, stroking it. He moved his hand away. "You're anything but boring. And this average shit is getting on my nerves. Honey, you are so far above average, average can't even see you unless it looks up with a telescope." Nate sighed. "I have wanted to meet a boring guy like you for so long I was beginning to think you didn't even exist."

"And here I am."

"And here you are."

Brandon leaned in to kiss him, and Nate pulled back. "You sure you want to do that?"

Brandon planted a chaste kiss on Nate's lips. "It's going to take a lot more than a little puke to keep me away from you, Mr. Tippie." He winked. "Although I will wait for a more passionate kiss until you've had a chance to brush."

Brandon pulled the quilt up tighter around Nate's shoulders. "You should try to sleep. Rest will bring you back." He leaned over to shut off the light and then made to move off the bed.

"Where are you going?" Nate asked.

"I was going to make up the couch, give you your space."

"I don't need my space. I thought you were going to take care of me. I promise I'll make it into the john if I have to hurl again."

"Oh, what a sweet talker you are!" Brandon lay back down. "How could I resist such a romantic man?"

Brandon wriggled his hand beneath the covers so he could hold Nate's hand. They fell asleep that way.

*

Nate awakened in the morning, alone and feeling completely recovered. Sunlight poured into the room, and the first thing he did was turn to look for Brandon. But the bed was empty.

There was a note beside the bed.

*Punkin,*

*I went over to Nancy's to take her to church and breakfast. Yeah, I'm that kind of wild man. You looked so cute sleeping there—and it was good to see you were at peace and your color had come back. Feel free to help yourself to the kitchen if you're up for it. There are bagels, cream cheese, tea, coffee, cereal. Take whatever you want. Just make sure the door is locked when you leave.*

*Or—don't leave. Stay here and surprise me in bed, naked, when I get home.*

*Brandon*

Nate set the note back on the nightstand. "What the hell did I ever do to deserve you?" He shook his head and sat up, placing his legs on the bamboo floor, testing. He felt fine. It was amazing to him that he could have felt so awful the night before and so good this morning.

Wishing Brandon were still there, he reached down and rubbed at his customary morning wood.

Maybe Nate would take him up on that offer to be here when he got home. Grinning, he slipped from the bed and went in search of coffee.

# Chapter Thirteen

Hannah slid into her jeans and smock, pulled a brush through her red hair, and applied a little lip gloss. What she loved about working at the animal hospital was that she didn't have to dress up, and it took so little effort to get ready for work in the morning. Sundays, especially, were quieter, with the clinic only open until two.

Once she slid into her Nikes, she was all ready to face the day.

Heading out of her bedroom, she thought she'd check on her brother before she left. She hurried up the stairs, both anticipating and dreading what she would find. She knocked and, when there was no answer, pushed open the door.

Nate's room was, as usual, tidy and...empty.

Hannah shook her head, feeling a potent mix of jealousy, despair, anger, and loss radiate through her. She wished now she hadn't bothered to look.

She pulled the door behind her and headed back downstairs. She had just enough time for a couple of pieces of toast and a cup of tea, but she wasn't hungry. Instead, she sat at the dining room table and flipped open her laptop and pointed herself to OpenHeartOpenMind.

Nate didn't have any new messages, which wasn't surprising because she hadn't been active on the account in the last twenty-four hours. Hannah had learned that the emails and messages rose when "he" was online.

Still, a perverse impulse rose up within her, and she chose not to consider from whence it came.

She opened a fresh email message and began writing.

*Dear Sweet Brandon,*

*Last night was the best. I hope it won't bother you a lot when I admit to you that I have had many, many lovers—too many to count!*

*I say this not to make you jealous, my sweet, oh no. I say this to you now so you will know that you are the absolute best. Best top. Best cuddler. Best kisser. Best hugger. Best cocksucker. Best cocksuckee. You are everything I ever dreamed of in a man—and then some.*

*Last night, in your bed, in case you couldn't tell from my sighs and moans, you steered me straight to paradise with your mouth, your cock. As I said, I'm not inexperienced, but, honey, you brought me to heights of passion I never knew existed.*

*That's all. I just wanted to say, thank you. And I can't wait to feel you inside me again.*

*And, of course, have a nice day.*

*Your Nate*

Hannah read over what she had written, grinning. She could tell herself she was just helping the lovebirds along, propelling their romance to further heights of bliss.

But deep down she wondered if there wasn't some malice in the words she had written, especially talking about Nate's promiscuity. She really didn't know what

Nate had shared with Brandon and didn't know how that kind of past would go over with him.

*Oh well.* Hannah shrugged. *He needs to know who my brother is someday, sooner rather than later. Honesty is the best policy, right?* She snorted at that last thought.

She hit Send. As soon as she did it, she wished she hadn't.

How long could she maintain this ruse, this worming her way into her brother's love life? It was crazy and despicable, and Hannah knew, rationally, that what she was doing was dangerous and dishonest.

It was so unlike her. It seemed more like something Marilyn would do.

She had been about to head out into the morning sunshine to walk the few blocks it would take her to get to the clinic. She enjoyed her "commute," especially on summer days like this one, with the air still retaining a hint of night's chill being rapidly burned off by the sun, when it was quiet.

But now, she felt a little sick. She sat down hard in a dining room chair and lowered her head into her hands.

*Why are you doing this?*

*Writing these notes is what a crazy person would do. It's kind of stalker-esque.*

*It's sick.*

*Why are you doing this?*

And Hannah forced herself to really face that question. She knew the answer, had known it all along.

*It's because you're alone. And maybe always will be. While your brother, your handsome, happy-go-lucky brother, has a bumper crop of men, more than he can handle. And you can't find even one.*

*You're jealous, Hannah. And it's not pretty.*

Pretty or not, Hannah realized if she didn't hustle, she would be late for work, and, in a time-card environment like the clinic, that was not something she wanted to be. She quickly logged out of OpenHeartOpenMind and headed for the door.

Just as she was locking the door, she heard her "Single Ladies" ringtone sounding from her bag. She opened the bag and pulled out her phone.

Unknown caller. Hannah considered letting it go to voice mail, but she thought she was perfectly capable of walking and talking at the same time. It was probably a sales call or a wrong number, anyway. Her phone was about as quiet these days as Marcel Marceau.

She hit Accept and started down the street. "Hello."

"Hey, Hannah. It's me."

A man was calling her. And it wasn't a wrong number, since he knew her name. Hannah's bad mood started to lift, like the bank of fog hanging over Green Lake right now. "Who's me?"

"Walt. Walt Briggs? We met on Friday, at Union?"

*And you said he'd never call.* Hannah grinned. "Hi, Walt! What's going on?"

"I hope it's not too early."

"Nope, no, I was just on my way to work. I work at a vet clinic, Aloha Dog and Cat?"

Walt chuckled. "I bring my Brussels Griffon there—Miriam. Are you a vet?"

"No, I just work at the front desk. We've probably met before." Hannah knew she'd be pulling Miriam's chart as soon as she got to work.

"Anyway," Walt said, "I won't keep you. I was just on my way out the door with Miriam, for her morning constitutional. I just wanted to say how nice it was meeting you. I, uh, was wondering if you might be available one night this week for dinner?"

Hannah was so rusty. It had been a long time. "Are you asking me out on a date?"

Walt laughed. "Well, yeah, that was the general idea. I'm hoping you'll say yes."

"Yes." Hannah's response practically overlapped Walt's own "yes." "So when are you thinking?"

"How about Tuesday? Wednesday? I know a great little Mexican spot in Ballard, Señor Moose."

Hannah's bad mood had now completely evaporated. She was smiling as she walked along the sun-dappled streets. "Let's make it sooner, Walt. Tuesday?"

"I'll pick you up at seven."

Hannah gave him her address, and the two confirmed they were both looking forward to the evening before hanging up.

Suddenly, what her brother was doing last night didn't seem so interesting to her.

*Wait until Marilyn hears this!* Hannah picked up her pace.

*

"I'll be right out, Nan!" Brandon called over his shoulder. He was in Nancy's guest room, at the glass-topped desk she had positioned at a window overlooking a wooded ravine. "I just wanna check my email."

"Good Lord, can't you young people go an hour without being online?" Nancy yelled from the kitchen, where she was scrambling eggs.

"Guess not, Mother dear. Won't take me a sec." Brandon signed in to OpenHeartOpenMind. He had to check. He had left Nate all alone that morning and wanted to see if he got his note and to see how he was. Of course, he knew he could simply pick up the phone and call, or even text, but if Nate was still sleeping, he didn't want to disturb him. He had looked so peaceful when Brandon had left that morning, like an angel, like an innocent child.

Brandon could have stared at him for hours, even if there were other impulses, not so childish, not so angelic, coursing through him as he looked at the handsome face in slumber on his own pillow.

He set the coffee his mom had made next to the keyboard and opened OpenHeartOpenMind.

Yea! There was a message from Nate.

He began reading.

He read the message again.

A third time.

He shook his head. What was going on? No longer could he pretend these mistakes in Nate's messages were simply fantasies or errors. He didn't know what game Nate was playing, but it was profoundly disturbing.

He felt his own queasiness in the pit of his gut.

He hit reply and typed:

*Why are you doing this? It makes no sense.*

He hit Send.

He wished he could get up and leave his mom's at this very moment, hurry home and confront Nate, find out just what the hell was going on. But he couldn't just rush out of her house, leaving the woman with a breakfast for two before her. How selfish!

"Brandon? The eggs are going to get cold."

Brandon said, "Be right out."

It was going to be a long breakfast.

He closed OpenHeartOpenMind and, for a moment, wishing he had never heard of the site.

*

The simple meal passed in what seemed like hours and hours—like a full day. By the time Brandon got himself ready to leave and kissed Nancy goodbye, he felt as though he had been at her house forever, going through eating the breakfast she had made—the eggs with diced ham, the sourdough bread smeared with her homemade peach butter—with feigned enthusiasm—hell, with feigned hunger. Every time he looked up at the clock on the kitchen wall, expecting to see fifteen minutes or so had passed, it would reveal that, in actuality, only two or three minutes had transpired.

Now, on the short bus ride home, he wished he could sit behind the driver, tapping him on the shoulder, urging him to break the speed limit, run yellow lights, ignore that woman who had to hold everything up by putting her bike in the holder on the front.

The odds were good that Nate wouldn't be there. Surely, there were things the man would have to do today, even though Brandon had no idea what those things might be.

Who was Nate Tippie, anyway?

Brandon wasn't sure he knew anymore, and it just about broke his heart.

He recalled his note from that morning that hinted Nate should stay and wait for him to come home. It was a pipe dream, a romantic fantasy, but now Brandon hoped he had taken the message to heart. But he had to admit, in his state of confusion and disappointment, he was no longer so eager to come home and find Nate in bed, naked, waiting for him.

There would be no more sex until things got cleared up. The sad thing was, Brandon had no idea how they could be, because he didn't know what the fuck was going on. For the life of him, he couldn't think of a rational explanation for the strange messages.

He ran the block from his bus stop to his apartment near the water, his heart racing for reasons entirely independent of his fleetness of foot.

Fitting his key into the lock, he listened for sounds, movement. He cocked his head because he heard music. He recognized the plaintive voice of Loreena McKennitt, singing something sad and, yes, romantic.

He opened the door, and the wall of sound, so soft and lush, greeted him. The living room and breakfast bar were glowing with flickering light—candles in glass holders had been lit. Brandon looked down to see a trail of red rose petals on his hardwood floor, leading back to his bedroom. In spite of himself, he grinned and followed.

The bedroom had been decked out in candles as well. Nate must have gone shopping. Nearly every surface held a candle, casting flickering illumination and scent into the air.

Nate lay in the middle of the bed, naked and smiling, surrounded by rose petals. Their sweet scent competed with the candles. Brandon watched as Nate's dick awakened, enticed by Brandon's arrival, and stood to greet him politely.

Brandon wished he had never opened the email this morning, wished he could experience the joy he knew he'd otherwise feel at this moment, the joy and the passion.

But the confusion of Nate's email nagged at him, and he wished, more than ever, he could summon some logical reason for what he had written.

But he could not.

And he had to know.

Brandon set the bag of leftovers Nancy had sent him home with down on the floor, not saying a word. He smiled at Nate, but there was something sad in his expression. Nate looked at him, suddenly wary. His cock, at full mast, began to sag.

Brandon moved around the room, methodically blowing out the candles and hoping that, once the situation had been explained, he could relight them and somehow reignite the passion this lovely situation foretold.

At last he sat on the bed next to Nate. Nate pulled a sheet up to cover himself and leaned back against the headboard. He was the first to speak. "So what's going on, Brandon?"

Brandon gently touched Nate's leg beneath the sheet, then pulled his hand away. "Funny. That's just the question I had for you."

"I don't understand."

"What you wrote to me this morning—all about our passionate night last night. I'm sorry to be dense, but I didn't get it."

Nate didn't say anything for a long time. "Honey, what are you talking about? I didn't write to you."

Brandon got up, crossed to his dresser, and grabbed his iPad from its surface. He brought up the OpenHeartOpenMind site, logged in, and went to his email. The message, like a coiled snake, was, of course, still there.

Returning to the bed, he held out the tablet, waiting for Nate to take it.

He watched as Nate's eyes quickly scanned the message. He looked up at Brandon, and Brandon could see the confusion and wariness stamped on Nate's features. "I didn't write this."

Brandon was suddenly relieved. Why hadn't he thought of this before? Someone else had access to Nate's account. That made sense. Perhaps there was a jealous, spurned boyfriend in the wings who had somehow gotten hold of Nate's password, knew about Nate and Brandon, and was now trying to fuck things up. He shook his head, thinking that, if that were the case, this spurned lover certainly had an odd way of going about things.

But it wasn't for him to figure out the logic of a stranger. Brandon felt like he knew truth when he saw it, and he could see truth on Nate's features when he read the message. He looked as genuinely befuddled by the message as Brandon had felt when he had read it that morning.

"What do you think it means?" Brandon asked, feeling a kind of relief course through him. Maybe things would be all right after all.

"Oh, I know what it means." Nate's lips compressed into a thin, angry line.

"You do?"

"Yeah. I know who wrote this." Nate shifted his gaze upward, as though praying for deliverance.

Brandon was insecure once more. He didn't like the fact Nate knew something about this, even if he didn't write the message.

"Who?" Brandon asked. "Some jealous boyfriend?" Sickness rose up within him, and he tasted a splash of bile at the back of his throat. Was Nate now going to reveal to him that he had a boyfriend or, even worse, a husband? This was, after all, Washington State. He glanced down at Nate's perfect hands but found no rings on any of its fingers.

Nate laughed. "Oh, there may be some jealousy, but this was written by no boyfriend. And—by the way—I have no boyfriend, just to set the record straight. Although I was hoping to cast someone who shall remain nameless in the role very soon." Nate winked at him.

But Brandon was too flustered to summon even the glimmer of a smile in response. "I don't understand. This is your account, isn't it?"

"Yes...and no." Nate blew out a sigh and said the words lovers everywhere have always dreaded: "We need to talk."

"Tell me."

"Okay, first the big reveal. The person who wrote you that message is—don't be too shocked—my sister, Hannah."

"The one you live with?"

Nate nodded. "The one and only. She's it as far as siblings go."

"Wait. Your sister wrote me a message, pretending to be you, about us having sex? That's bizarre."

"Tell me about it. My sister's a nice enough woman, but she's lonely. I think she probably wanted to share in my good fortune in finding you, sick as that sounds."

"Is your sister crazy? In and out of institutions? Substance-abuse issues?"

Nate laughed. "Don't you diss my Hannah! She has her quirks, but I still love her. You have to meet her."

"No way, dude." Brandon recoiled.

"Don't be that way." Nate went quiet.

They both sat, frozen, on the bed for a long time. Brandon realized it was early enough in their relationship—if it could even be called that—for the budding romance to wither on the vine.

And that made him sad. He told himself that Nate had no control over his sister, who must be a very strange character indeed. The kind his mom would say was a few bricks short of a load. But, again, it wasn't Nate's fault, was it, if his sister acted bizarrely?

Then he had a thought. "How did she get access to your account?" He expected Nate to reply with something about a simple password, or automatic sign in, or even that he always left his computer on and never signed out of anything.

But that was not the answer he gave.

"This is why we need to talk. See…" Nate drew in a deep breath, his gaze making a circuit around the bedroom, never coming to rest on Brandon's own questioning eyes. "It's not my account," he said at last, in a rush.

"What?"

Nate told Brandon about Hannah and her friend Marilyn—their drunken escapade when they created the online persona of Whos2Know and attached his picture to it.

Brandon bit his lower lip and asked, "So you never wrote any of those messages to me?"

Nate shook his head. "I'm sorry."

"Did you pick the picture?" Somewhere inside of him, Brandon hoped, in a weird way, that Nate *did* have some connection to the profile.

"No. But it was a good one, huh?" Nate grinned, but the smile withered as quickly as it came.

Brandon was not smiling. "So…the profile. You didn't write it?"

"No, I'm so sorry. But I'm here now."

Brandon wished he could return Nate's hopeful smile, but he was just too weirded out by all of this. "How did you end up getting involved?"

Brandon watched as Nate swallowed hard. "It was Hannah. She asked me to meet you. She liked you a lot, Brandon. And she didn't want to just pull the profile with no word, so she asked me to meet up with you to let you down gently."

Brandon stood, no longer wanting to occupy the same bed.

"But, honey," Nate said. "When I met you, I was head over heels. Really. Please come back and sit here beside me."

"I need time to process this," Brandon said to the wall. He couldn't bear to look at Nate. Heat burned his cheeks. He felt like such a fool.

"Brandon...come on. The ends justify the means, right? We met, and I really like you, maybe even something more."

Brandon let a shaky sigh escape his lips. "I don't know about that. I don't know about any of this." He moved to the window, where he looked out at the lakefront and all the people on its trails—the runners, bikers, people walking their dogs—and felt very much removed from them.

He heard the creak of the bed as Nate got off of it and came up behind him. He placed tentative hands on Brandon's shoulders. Brandon, without thinking, shrugged them off. He turned and looked at Nate, this gorgeous man standing before him, completely naked and vulnerable, and said, "I need you to go."

"Oh, don't be this way. I had nothing to do with all of this."

"That's just it. Please, Nate, don't make me yell at you." Brandon turned back to staring out the window, listening as Nate hurriedly gathered up his things. He heard him struggling into his clothes, heard his quick pace to the front door, heard him say, "Call me, okay? We'll figure this out. I don't want to lose you. Please, Brandon."

Brandon never looked at him, couldn't respond.

He winced as he heard the door close. When he spotted Nate on the street below, Nate turned to look up at him. Even from up here, Brandon could see his eyes were plaintive, begging.

Brandon moved back into the shadows.

# Chapter Fourteen

Nate looked up at the minimalist, environmentally conscious town house he shared with his sister. When they had bought it several years ago, he thought it would be a happy—but temporary—place for the two of them, a sanctuary where they could be together, each other's only immediate family. Now its geometric planes, umber and orange exterior, simply looked cold, the bamboo stark instead of warm and inviting.

Nate had had high hopes that, one day in the not-too-distant future, they would sell the place because one or both of them had found someone else with whom he or she would like to live. It was only natural that they would eventually pair off with someone special.

Yet a part of him feared they would wind up senior citizens, sharing a home and a few cats, bickering over the last of the high blood pressure medicine in the cabinet and looking more and more like twins.

And now that Nate had at last found someone special, amid all the years of meaningless hooking up, the disappointing dates, the halfhearted attempts to make a relationship work when there had been no spark, Nate felt as though he was on the verge of losing him, practically before he'd had him.

And why? Because of a meddling sister? How could that be? On his way over, after the bus had dropped him off on Broadway, he thought of the irony that the same duplicity and cyber manipulations that had brought him to Brandon were the same ones that now could rip them apart.

Nate felt a mixture of emotions—sadness, anxiety, and a slow-boiling rage. He didn't know if, in his current state, now was the right time to have a conversation with his sister, but knew that if he didn't, he just might lose his mind.

He hurried up the walk and went inside. He heard the TV go off when he opened the door. He came up the stairs into the living room, and there was Hannah, sitting on the couch, remote still in hand, grinning at him. "The prodigal brother comes home! Wow, by the length of time you've been gone, I assume you have had a very good time—and are most likely totally exhausted. No worries about dinner. I ordered pizza in from Pagliacci."

Nate didn't know what to say. She had no idea, sitting there on the couch, perhaps waiting to hear the sordid details about his night of heated passion with Brandon. He wished for a moment there was a way to rewind things so that the whole OpenHeartOpenMind episode had never happened.

*Yeah, but if that were the case, you might never have met Brandon.* He was sure that much was true. Yet if Hannah had just left things alone, everything would have been fine. And who knows? Maybe he would have met Brandon without the silly cybermanipulation. After all, their eyes had met when they were running, that one day around the lake. Who knew if that chance meeting would have repeated itself and, if it had, if either of them would have made a move to speak?

*Why was the world so complicated?*

*Why couldn't Hannah have stopped at creating the profile and left it alone after he and Brandon had met? There would have been no harm done.* He hung his head in despair. Was everything going to be ruined now? Would association with his sister taint him? Could Brandon ever trust him? And what was a relationship without trust, one built on duplicity?

He shook his head. He didn't know.

"Nate? Are you okay? Say something."

He took the last two steps into the living room and took a seat near his sister on the couch.

"Remember when we were kids and that bully—what his name?—something hick-like. Junior? Remember how he was going to beat me up that time? All the kids in the neighborhood had gathered around to watch the sissy get pounded on. And Junior was taunting me, telling me how he was going to kick the crap out of me. I remember standing there, so scared, just waiting for it to happen, to take the pain of the blows, for it to be over."

Nate smiled sadly at his sister.

"Then I looked up, and there you were, walking down the street toward us. I remember you had on the black-and-white checked coat that went so well with your red hair. I remember the bare trees and the light of dusk. It was early spring."

"Nate? What are you talking about?"

"I remember...feeling safe. You were my savior. One of the kids must have run off to our house and told our mom what was about to happen. And you, Hannah, you were not about to let it." Nate felt, weirdly, his eyes well with tears at the memory. He pushed at them with the back of his hand. "When I saw you coming down that street, I don't know if I'd ever felt more loved and protected. I do know that I had never loved my big sister more.

"You saved me that day, chased the bully off and brought you home. Don't you remember?"

Hannah nodded. "Yeah, I think I do now."

Nate sat with her in silence. The memory had taken the edge off his anger. It had always been that way. Hannah was the older one, the protector. Was what she had done a part of that?

"Hannah, why?"

He looked over at her, meeting her eyes.

"Why what?" she asked, but Nate could see she looked anxious. She toyed with a loose thread at the bottom of her sweatshirt.

"Why did you continue writing to Brandon?"

Nate watched, and he knew his sister realized she was busted. Her fair skin went from pale to scarlet in fewer than ten seconds. She couldn't look at him. "Why? Did something happen?"

"Yeah. We were getting along great until you interfered. Now I don't know if he wants to see me again."

"Oh no! That can't be. All I wrote was what I'm sure happened. I was just hoping to push the two of you closer." Hannah laughed, but it was breathless, verging close to hysteria.

"Really, Hannah? Then why that crack about how many guys I've had? Sure, it's true, and I'm not ashamed of it, but do you think that's something Brandon would enjoy hearing—about someone maybe he was just beginning to care for?"

"Well, maybe that wasn't the brightest thing to put in there. I'm sorry, Nate. Was he mad about that? I only meant to show how special Brandon was to you. Good intentions, you know?"

Nate shook his head. "I don't know if he was mad about that. Single gay men—most of us are tomcats at one point or another. What he was mad about was that you wrote to him, that you were behind all of this."

Hannah shook her head. "I don't understand. You told him?"

"I had to!" Nate shouted, and Hannah leaned back into the couch, recoiling as if he had raised a hand to strike her.

"Why?"

"Because the little night of passion you wrote about never happened. It was weird, Sis, weird and sick."

"But you've been gone almost twenty-four hours. I figured it was a pretty safe bet you were just doing what came naturally."

Nate blew out an exasperated breath. "I was sick, Hannah. We went out to dinner last night, and I got food poisoning. Brandon and I didn't fuck last night. He took care of me, put me to bed, made me tea, and didn't get grossed out when I puked. I was sure this was a man I could love." Nate stood and went to stare out the front window at the traffic passing by on their street. His voice barely above a whisper, he said, "And now I think that's ruined."

He turned back to Hannah. "I had to tell him everything, Hannah. All about the profile, why I met him the first time, the other notes I guess you wrote to him." He shook his head. "I don't understand it. Why did you keep writing? Why didn't you at least tell me?"

Hannah didn't say anything for a long time. "I don't know. Or maybe I do know and don't want to face it."

Nate turned to regard his sister.

Hannah rubbed at her thighs, curled a lock of hair between her fingers. "You have it all. Men run after you like...like dogs after a bone, like cats after cream, like a Fundamentalist Christian after a boycott." She looked up at her brother, and her eyes glistened. She shrugged. "I liked Brandon too. I liked how he looked. I liked the words he put on the page. I liked that he seemed quiet, kind, nurturing."

Hannah swallowed, and it seemed as though she could not meet her brother's gaze. "Brandon seemed like the kind of guy I'd always hoped *I'd* meet. It seems like all I ever get—when I get anyone at all—are losers, guys who don't want to commit, liars, married men, guys who are way too into their mothers, or their cars, or online porn. Guys who I think I had a wonderful time with, and then they never call again. Guys who find someone younger, or cuter, or who's willing to do anal." She snorted with laughter, but it had an edge of bitterness to it. "*Now* I know your secret!"

"Sis, I didn't know."

"What? You thought I sat around here on the weekends with Marilyn by choice, that watching an old weeper with her and a bottle of wine was just one of my many options?" Hannah shook her head.

"It just seemed like when he wrote to me—and I know, I know he was really writing to you—he spoke to a place deep within me. If it doesn't sound too corny, he touched my heart."

"It does sound too corny." Nate sat down next to his sister.

Hannah went on. "I don't care. I just wanted to keep the conversation going." Hannah stared straight ahead, and Nate saw the tears standing in her eyes, waiting to fall. She had always been the one he looked up to, the one he always thought could take care of herself. He had been too busy with his own love life, or sex life, or whatever you want to call it, to realize she didn't have one of her own. And here she was, pushing forty and pretending to be a gay man as she fell head over heels for a guy who didn't even know she existed.

It was all so sad.

Nate moved forward, gathered Hannah up in his arms, and drew her in close. He stroked her thick red hair and whispered, "You know, I think I get it. And I'm sorry that you've been lonely. Sorry that I haven't really noticed."

Hannah wept into his chest for a few minutes, then drew in a great quivering breath and pulled away from him. He could see how she forced herself to smile, wiping the tears from the corners of her eyes. "Enough of this pity party! For Christ's sake. I'm the one who should be saying 'I'm sorry,' and I am. I do. Whatever."

Hannah touched Nate's cheek tenderly. "I apologize. I had no business doing what I did. I just, just wanted to be close to him, you know?"

Nate thought of Brandon, sitting on the bed next to him, stroking his forehead when he was sick, thought of him at dinner before, the way he pulled out the chair for his mom, thought of him in bed, moving in to kiss him. "Yeah," he said softly. "I know."

"I won't do it again," Hannah said. "I'll delete the account, and I'll apologize to him."

"I don't know if that's such a good idea right now." Nate remembered the dull, quiet rage and hurt he could feel radiating off Brandon when he left him. If he had bad feelings toward Nate, he couldn't imagine what Brandon thought of his sister.

"Delete the account—and don't ever do anything like this again."

"I won't, Nate, I promise. It was just a lark that got out of hand."

Nate nodded. He was thinking of how that lark had brought him close to someone with whom he believed he could have fallen in love, maybe someone with whom he could have begun to build a future.

And how that lark ruined everything.

Would he ever see Brandon again? Or would this nonsense be like a wall between them, now separating them forever?

The pizza arrived, and they busied themselves getting out plates, paper napkins, Tabasco, grated cheese, and Cokes. When they were settled in front of the TV, Hannah told Nate something else, something he guessed she thought might make him happy—and it did—but it also made him feel lower than before.

"Guess what? I have a date Tuesday night!"

"Really?" Nate shifted a mouthful of pizza to one corner of his mouth. "Who with? And when did this come about?"

Hannah told him about being at Union on Friday night.

"You were there when I was?" Nate set his pizza down and stared at his sister, head cocked. "Why didn't you say anything?"

"I was spying. I wanted to make sure you were following my instructions."

"You spied on me? You didn't trust me to do what you asked?"

"Good thing, huh? Because you sure as hell didn't!" Hannah laughed, but Nate did not join in.

Suddenly, the pizza didn't taste good anymore. "I'm going to bed." He took his plate out to the kitchen, dumped the half-eaten slice in the trash, then rinsed the plate and left it on the counter. He started up the stairs.

"Nate? What's the matter?"

"Nothing." Nate continued upward. "Nothing at all."

In his room, he tried calling Brandon, but the call went to voice mail.

In the living room, Hannah was making her own phone call. When Marilyn picked up at the other end, she said, "We have to make this right."

Marilyn wondered, "Make what right? Our lesbian love? The situation in the Middle East? Legalization of marijuana? Oh wait, we already did that."

Hannah rolled her eyes and made no comment. Instead, she told Marilyn the whole story about the letters to Brandon and how she had, of course, been rapidly exposed. "And now everything's a mess. The guy, who seemed so cute and nice, now wants nothing to do with my brother because of me. We have to make it right."

"Did you ever know that you're my hero?" Marilyn barked out a short laugh.

"What? We're referencing female buddy movies now?"

"Yeah, you're my hero because I don't think I could have dreamed up a crazier bitch for a best friend. I mean, I read to escape, but no one in my books ever comes close to the drama and shit you get yourself into, girlfriend."

"Well, thank you very much. But enough flattery—if that's what we're calling it. What should we do about this thing between Nate and Brandon? How do we fix it?"

"We don't."

"Huh?"

"Honey, haven't you learned anything? You've meddled enough. Anything you do directly from here on out is only gonna make things worse. And you risk alienating not only dreamboat over there in Green Lake, but your brother too. Leave it alone. Let the boys work things out themselves."

"But it's my fault that they even have anything to work out."

"You're right. And now the thing to do, the thing you should have done long before this, is to step away."

Hannah eyed her computer, which sat innocently on the dining room table. Where would be the harm in one more note to Brandon? Not from Nate, but from her? A sincere letter of apology and one that defended her brother, letting Brandon know he shouldn't take the blame for any of this. It was all her.

"Hannah? Are you listening?"

"Oh, I'm listening. And taking it all to heart." She changed the subject quickly. "Remember that guy from the bar? Walt?"

"Yeah."

"He asked me out. We're going to dinner on Tuesday."

"Well, there you go, then. You've got your own man to contend with. Good for you," Marilyn said, although it didn't sound to Hannah like she meant it. "Listen, I just downloaded the new BF Mann book, and I was in the middle of reading. Do you mind?"

"Not at all. I got some stuff I want to do before turning in anyway." Hannah eyed the computer again. "See you at work tomorrow."

*Dear Brandon,*

*My name is Hannah. I don't know if Nate told you my name, but I'm his sister. I guess you know by now that it was me who created the Whos2Know profile, and it was also me who wrote to you.*

*I wanted to write you one more time before I backed away from the mess I've made, just to tell you I'm sorry. I won't go into the reasons I did what I did. But I will say that I could tell, even from our very brief correspondence, that you are a terrific man, the kind of man who, if you were differently inclined, I'd like to have in my own life. I enjoyed talking and flirting with you! I hope you don't think that's too strange.*

*Okay, you probably do. I deserve it.*

*I am sorry, though, and I wanted you to know that any discomfort or anger you're feeling about this situation should lie entirely in my lap. Not my brother's. Brandon, he's nuts about you. He thinks you're the cat's meow.*

*I know I wrote that kind of bitchy thing about all the guys he's been involved with, and I'm sorry for that too. My brother is a great guy, and while it's true he's dated quite a few fellas, it's also true that I have never seen one affect him as much as you did.*

*So please don't hold any bad feelings you might have against him. He's a good guy. And so are you.*

*You deserve to be together.*

*Best regards,*

*Hannah*

Hannah read over what she had written. The email was honest and forthright, and she prayed it would do some good.

She hit Send.

# Chapter Fifteen

Brandon got up for work the next morning feeling as if something had been sucked out of him; he didn't know what. It was as though all his vitality was gone. His life force—his energy. When Nate walked out Brandon's front door, he had taken it all with him.

He sat up in bed, then pulled on a pair of nylon shorts, a tank top, and his Nikes. He did a few perfunctory stretches and headed outside. Even though he felt drained, running would restore his energy and give him some peace of mind.

It always did.

It was only a little after six, and the sun had just risen. Green Lake was relatively quiet. There were a few walkers and runners, but the path around the water was as serene as the water itself, quiescent, a mirror. A cool breeze buffeted his body.

He tried to concentrate on his breathing, but his thoughts always went back to Nate. Why did what happened have to happen? Things had been going so well! But how could he build something with the man when the foundation was so shaky? Brandon realized it was all Nate's sister's doing, but still, Nate had gone along with it. Nate had known—and he never bothered to let Brandon in on it.

And that made him wonder if there was anything else Nate hadn't let him in on. Would he worry, if they did stay together, what else Nate was hiding from him?

He couldn't be with a liar. He thought of one of the last guys he had dated, a few months ago, someone who also seemed really nice: a bearded guy named Gary who lived at the top of Queen Anne hill. Gary was great, Brandon remembered, because he did something so few men could do—make him laugh. He just had a way of looking at the world that was both absurd and ticklish. Brandon had had high hopes for him as well.

But then he and Gary were just about to go to bed for the first time. And that was when things stopped being so funny, because Brandon had asked, before things got too involved, a critical question.

"Everything okay with you?"

Gary had looked at him quizzically, pulling down the comforter on the bed. "Yup. Why?"

But Brandon had seen a flicker of doubt cross Gary's otherwise affable features.

"Healthwise."

Gary had removed his hand completely then. "Well, I am poz, if that's what you're asking."

It was then Brandon had known that Gary might never have told him if he hadn't asked. Dishonesty like Gary's was dangerous, never mind duplicitous. Selfish.

Brandon didn't need lies.

Brandon didn't know if it was worth it to continue with a man he wasn't sure he could trust. It was still early days—*way* early days—with the two of them. The fact of the matter was, as much as it hurt, it would be better to make a clean break and move on.

There was someone else out there for him, Brandon was sure, who didn't come with a ton of baggage, a passel of lies. Honesty and integrity—those were qualities that far outlasted blond hair, blue eyes, and muscles.

*And a thick, perfect dick that didn't know when to quit. Don't forget that.*

Brandon stopped, amazed he had already made it around the lake once, a distance of three miles. He bent over, hands on knees, gasping. He had run the distance in a little over twenty minutes, which was pretty fast for him. Maybe if he kept his mind occupied with romance troubles, he could win some races. He laughed and began heading home. He'd stop at Peet's on the way to pick up a hibiscus iced tea.

At home, he sat down with his tea at his computer and signed in to OpenHeartOpenMind. He might as well plow through all the other emails that had come in before and during his brief time with Nate. He could begin looking for some new candidates. It's what he figured his mom would tell him to do, anyway.

And mom was always right.

When he opened his messages, his heart about stopped. The most recent one was from Whos2Know. It made him feel a quick surge of anger. What now? Were they both playing with him? Was he being punked, the centerpiece of some elaborate joke only Nate and his sister could understand?

He was tempted to simply check the box next to the message and then click on the wastebasket icon. Enough was enough.

But, human nature being what it is, Brandon couldn't do that. Even though he knew he was probably drawing himself into something unhealthy, he opened the message.

He read it over. At least it was honest. At least it wasn't her trying to pretend to be her brother. But it was still strange. He still didn't like it.

But Hannah had made a point—Nate really had little to do with this whole mess. And maybe all Brandon had needed was for someone to say that to him.

Brandon left the computer. He wanted to get away from its power to confuse him. He wished, kind of, that he had never posted the profile. His mother had been right when she gently suggested that maybe there were better ways to meet people than online. At least in the real world, you could trust your own eyes a little more.

He stripped out of his sweaty running clothes and got into the shower. He turned under the hot spray, soaping himself and clearheaded enough to realize, suddenly, that his head and his heart were at war. His head, of course, was telling him to move on, that Nate and this Hannah woman raised all sorts of red flags. His head continued, in its hectoring, know-it-all way, telling him that he had invested very little, and thus had nothing to lose by getting the hell away from these crazy people. His head added that Brandon should do something he had always told himself he should—join the gay running club, the Front Runners. After all, they met every Saturday morning at Green Lake for a get-together and run. He might meet a nice guy there. It was just that Brandon liked to run alone. It was like meditation for him.

This last thought led him to what his heart told him. His heart told him that people were human, that Hannah, misguided as she was, really didn't mean any harm. Now, he had no idea what the woman did mean, but he didn't think there was any malice in what she had done. He thought about the messages he had exchanged with her and realized that what was between the lines was a nice person who seemed to genuinely like him, that she was perhaps a lonely woman who found herself caught up in a connection that went further than she had intended.

And his heart was just full of images of Nate: his big blue eyes, his laugh, his hands and mouth—the things they could do to him. His heart reminded him of how good he felt when he was with Nate, not just in bed, although that was great, better than anything he'd ever experienced, but when they were just talking—how safe and appreciated Nate had made him feel.

Being with Nate was like coming home.

Brandon slipped out of the shower, turned it off, and reached for a towel. He shook his head, and a little laugh escaped his lips. The heart won out over the head every time.

Naked, he padded back to the computer and did a rash thing, but the action was one Brandon felt was warranted. OpenHeartOpenMind was still open. He moved his mouse up so he could click on the drop down for "Account." Once there, he clicked on "Delete Account." A message popped up, asking him if he was sure and telling him that all his favorites, buddies, messages, and preferences would be wiped out.

He clicked on "Yes, I'm sure," and, just like that, his account was history. Brandon felt a sense of relief wash over him. From here on out, it would be human contact the old-fashioned way—where you met an eye, heard a voice, felt a real human touch.

He was glad to see the account gone and, with it, the mysterious promise of the other men who had written to him. He wanted to see things through with Nate and intended to—gasp—call him when he got home from work, see if he might want to come over to his place for dinner. Brandon could throw together a pretty mean chicken stir-fry.

He dressed for work, humming, secure in the knowledge everything was going to be okay.

\*

Before Hannah headed out for work that morning, she thought she might as well check OpenHeartOpenMind to see if Brandon had responded to her. She hoped he had. It would be their first real exchange with no pretense. She would write him back and let him know that it was for the best that she close the Whos2Know account, now that the truth was out.

But when she logged into the site, she was stunned to find that Brandon was gone. She was told, in cold, bald terms, that Brandon's account had been deleted.

"Shit," Hannah whispered. She felt as though she already knew why—her message had only angered the guy further. Naturally, he wanted to get as far from her and Nate as possible. She tried to comfort herself with the knowledge that her apology probably hadn't made anything worse, that Brandon would have done the same with or without it. Still, it made her ache inside for her brother.

Speaking of her brother, he was just coming down the stairs, dressed in an oversized Elephant Car Wash T-shirt and flannel boxer shorts. His hair was mussed.

"You don't look like you had a good night's sleep."

"You're very observant this morning."

"Worried about what happened with Brandon?"

"No, Hannah, I was worried about what Madonna will do when she reaches retirement age. Do you think she's put enough aside?"

"I'm sorry! I guess I have a flair for the obvious. And, again, I do apologize for screwing things up." She wished she could say there was still hope, but she wasn't sure she had that optimism to give.

Nate blew out a sigh and went into the kitchen to grab a mug of coffee. "What's done is done."

Hannah gathered up her stuff to leave for the day. She might as well come out with it. "There's something you should know."

"What?" Nate all but glared at her.

"I wrote to him last night."

"Oh, Hannah! You didn't!"

"I just wanted to apologize."

"You should have stayed out of it."

"I know. I know you're right."

Nate took his coffee and sat down in the living room, not drinking it, just staring straight ahead. "Well? Is there more?"

"Um, yeah." Hannah edged to the front door. "I got up this morning to see if he had responded, and I noticed that he had deleted his account."

"Oh, that's great. I can hear the resounding slam of the virtual door in my face."

"I'm sorry, Nate," Hannah repeated.

"I'm the one who's sorry. Who knows if I'll ever meet a guy like Brandon again?"

"Oh, come on, now. Go look in the mirror. You've always had them crawling all over you."

"Don't you have to be at work?" Nate snapped.

Wordlessly, Hannah headed out into the morning.

\*

Nate sat on the couch for a long time, staring straight ahead, his coffee going cold before him. Drinking it would only increase the acid churning in his gut.

None of this would have happened, he thought, without deceit. Even if he had just told Brandon, the night they met, what his sister had been up to and what the original plan for their first date had been, all would probably be okay this morning.

Well, he was through with deceit. From here on out, he would be honest in every part of his life. Even if he never saw Brandon again, at least his life would be—quite literally—an open book.

Today would be a new beginning.

He stood and stretched, ready to head back up to his bedroom, his desk, and make a dramatic change.

Once upstairs, he tried to call Brandon one more time, hoping that this time would be the one where he'd get through. But the call, like the last several ones, went straight to voice mail. Nate had the sinking feeling that all of his calls to Brandon from now on would meet with the same fate.

It wasn't fair.

He set his phone down and opened his laptop. He logged into his website and opened the blog portion of it and began writing.

*I have an announcement to make. I am not the person you think I am. Today, I want you to meet the real me...*

Nate smiled as he typed in the words that followed quickly, as if they had been pent up inside of him for years, which, in fact, they had. There was a glorious sense of release and freedom as he opened up to his unseen readers' eyes.

He hoped they would still love him. He hoped he would still have a career. But that was a chance we all took when we laid ourselves open, becoming vulnerable. He really wouldn't be losing anything if they didn't love him, anyway, because what they had loved had been a figment of his imagination, nothing real.

Now they would know him, and it would be take it or leave it.

If he expected honesty from Hannah, he should expect no less from himself. He continued to type.

# Chapter Sixteen

Mondays, Marilyn had off. Unlike the majority of people she knew, Mondays were not a day to dread, but one to savor. She liked being able to get up late while the rest of the world groaned about starting the workweek, heading out into rush hour traffic, agonizing over the whole long week ahead of them. Somehow, it made her feel superior as she slept late and eased gently into her day, made a pot of Earl Grey for herself, and opened a can of Fancy Feast for her orange tabby, Mike. She could put up her feet.

Her apartment on Seventeenth Avenue in Capitol Hill was small but comfy and allowed her to get just about everywhere she wanted to go on foot. All the clubs and restaurants she would ever want to visit were just a stone's throw away. She liked the bustle of the neighborhood and how, no matter what hour she stepped outside, there were people about, and usually they were in good moods because they were having fun.

She had done her place up with what she thought of as lots of warm touches—things like scarves thrown over lamp shades, walls she had painted herself in a warm umber, wooden blinds and curtains at the windows, which looked down on the busy thoroughfare. She had decorated the walls with framed Herb Ritts posters, and the images of muscular men, captured in gloriously detailed black and white, never grew old. Her bedroom was dominated by her grandmother's four-poster, laid with a paisley-patterned down comforter and more throw pillows than she could count. In the center of the pillows sat Violet, a lavender and white teddy bear she had hung onto from her childhood. Next to Violet was Chuck, her best friend, a brown "leather bear" decked out in leather vest, chained harness, chaps, and biker cap.

She had just read a couple of chapters of the latest BF Mann novel and thought it would be very pleasant to spend the morning in bed, reading. She could finish the book by afternoon and then head over to Broadway for a bowl of chicken *pho* and some man watching. Reading gay romance always put her in a mood to ogle the boys. Fortunately for her, she lived in the perfect neighborhood to indulge this pastime. Broadway was like a runway for gay man flesh.

Indeed, Capitol Hill had gay men as far as the eye could see. Hell, she could scarcely swing Mike without hitting one.

But before she returned to her novel and its collection of steamy man-on-man sex, she thought she'd check out her Facebook account and see if anything, other than junk, lay in wait for her in her Gmail account.

A tempest was brewing among her Facebook friends, all of them big fans of the m/m romance genre. It seemed an announcement had gone out that morning that had just about gone viral, with everyone talking about it— endlessly. The comments jumped out at her.

*Can you believe it?*

*What on earth was he/she thinking? Why? Why? Why?*

*I'll never read him again!*

*I feel betrayed.*

*Come on, guys. The stories are still the same stories. I will stand by my "mann."*

When she saw what the fuss was about, Marilyn was taken aback. She went right to the writer-in-question's website to see if the brouhaha was true.

The author photo was what stunned her first, enough that her jaw dropped and she wasn't aware enough to close it. "Really?" she whispered to herself, and then said louder, "Really? Are you fucking kidding me?" Where once had been the picture of a fiftysomething woman with spiky red hair and glasses, now there was a thirtysomething man looking back at her—a man whose blond hair, dimples, and resemblance to actor Bradley Cooper were familiar.

Marilyn tittered, for the first time understanding the old cliché about not believing your own eyes. Her laughter was not born of amusement but was grounded firmly in disbelief, bordering on mild hysteria. How in the hell did *Nate* get his picture on author BF Mann's website? Marilyn stared hard at the photo, noticing that it was taken in Nate's bedroom office. She could see the bookcase over his right shoulder that she had admired the first time Hannah had given her the tour of the town house.

Marilyn laughed again, but it was more of a prickly laugh, an unpleasant sensation, evidence of her world being turned upside down.

She forced her eyes away from the photo and began reading the blog posted just beneath it.

*I have an announcement to make. I am not the person you think I am. Today, I want you to meet the real me: Nate Tippie, a thirty-four-year-old gay man living in Seattle, WA.*

*BF Mann, the woman you used to see on this website, the woman you believed wrote the books you love, is being put to rest today. She had a good run, but the old girl is tired and ready to hand over the reins to someone younger and a bit more chipper. Although I will continue to use the BF Mann pen name (it is, after all, my brand now), I wanted to come clean with my readers to let you know who I am.*

*Why? Well, there are many reasons, but the main one is that I no longer wanted to deceive you, even if deception was not in my heart when I started telling my little stories of two guys falling in love against suspenseful, paranormal, and sometimes horrific backdrops. I looked around me when my first book was published and noticed that many of my author peers were women and that many of them used gender-neutral names or names that began with initials. I wanted to be one of them. My thinking at the time, and my publisher agreed with me, was all about business. We both thought I'd sell more books to the ever-growing legion of straight women who loved gay romance if I was one of them.*

*So I became BF Mann, a spiky-haired, spunky redhead with a penchant for foul language and an appreciation for a rounded, bubblicious male tush.*

*Now, the real BF Mann shares those same qualities, especially the latter, which is why I can describe said tushes in such loving detail. And I think that by letting you know who I really am, you'll come to accept me. I am still the author of the stories you loved, the stories you bought in steadily increasing quantities over the years, enough to allow me to do what many artists can only dream about—make a living from my art.*

*I thank you for that and hope you will stick with me through my female-to-male transition. I have more stories locked up in this head than I will probably ever live to write, and I need you with me, conspiring to bring them to life.*

*I know you must have questions. First of all, those pictures of the redhead? Stock photos. I was always afraid you might run across them and expose me for the penis-wielding fool I am.*

*Now I no longer have to worry about that.*

*Getting back to what prompted me to come out of the closet, so to speak, as a gay man and not a straight woman writing about gay men—I am doing it for love. See, there's a whole backstory to this decision, one I won't bore you with and one I just might want to save for a future novel (wink). But recently, I met a terrific man, and our relationship has probably been ruined because of some not-so-innocent deception, deception not originated by me, but lies I should never have gone along with.*

*I don't want deception in my life anymore—not in any way, shape, or form. So I want you to know that BF Mann is a man, an out-and-proud gay man who is as hungry for love as his characters. I hope you will continue to love my stories even if right now you might be feeling, well, a little weird about me.*

*In the coming days and weeks, I will share more about my real life—photos, background. I will update my Facebook, Twitter, Pinterest, and Instagram with the new, real me.*

*And I do hope you'll drop me a line and let me know what you think. I hope you understand that this decision was born of a desire to not only be true to myself, but to you.*

BF Mann, or Nate, had left a link where readers could send him an email.

Marilyn sat for a long time, mouth open and staring. She couldn't process any thoughts, and thus her mind simply shut down. It wasn't until Mike came up to her and began winding his way between her legs, as he had a tendency to do, that the spell was broken.

"You son of a bitch," Marilyn whispered. The cat looked up. "Not you," she mumbled, patting him on the head. She wondered if she restarted her computer if the page would come up as it once had, with a woman nearly her own age at the helm of the BF Mann website. Had Marilyn stepped into some bizarre episode of *Twilight Zone*?

It wasn't so much that BF Mann was a man. Reading as she had so extensively in the m/m romance genre,

Marilyn knew it occurred fairly often that authors hid their genders behind masculine or indeterminate names. Some of the biggest names in the business had done it, and sometimes were outed with less-than-spectacular results, especially if the author in question had not only hid behind a name, but had created a whole persona to go with it. In cases like the latter, there had been fallout, but eventually readers always went back because, really, it was about the stories and not the man or woman behind the curtain, frantically pulling the levers.

But the thing that made this case different from most was the fact that this was not a woman masquerading as a gay man, but a gay man masquerading as a woman. Marilyn had to wonder what kind of strange universe she lived in, where such a charade would actually be more appealing than the truth. I mean, it seemed we would want our stories to come straight from the horse's, or the homosexual's, mouth, wouldn't we?

And yet, and yet... That wasn't always the case. Marilyn herself knew she took some comfort in knowing many of her favorite m/m romance authors were women, just like herself. While she never had consciously admitted it, she realized now she liked thinking she was part of some exclusive club of women, who both read and wrote man-on-man romance, who had a soft spot in their hearts (and maybe a wet spot farther south) for a gay kiss or some hot gay man lovin'. Like being gay itself, Marilyn reasoned, it was only natural.

So Hannah's brother was the real BF Mann and had been right under her nose this whole time? When a book had ended too abruptly for her taste, she could have quizzed him on what happened. She could have asked him for publication dates for upcoming books, gotten exclusive insider looks at cover art and works-in-progress. Hell, she could have pitched some of her own romance ideas his way, had she known.

The weird thing was that, naturally, she had never had any idea.

Did she feel deceived? Marilyn reached down and scooped up Mike to not only deposit him in her lap, but to get him to stop the infernal figure eights he was compulsively making between her legs. Did she feel deceived? Not really. She got that it was a business decision. She thought it was taking the deception a bit far to post pictures of some woman as himself. After all, was it really necessary to bring things to such a level? Plenty of authors didn't post photos of themselves, using instead avatars or book covers.

What Marilyn didn't like was that Nate had never shared the truth with her. She recalled many times when she had mentioned BF Mann's books to him and he showed no glimmer of recognition. Hannah would say, "Nate here isn't a big reader. He prefers to get between thousand-count sheets over paper ones."

He could have told her. They were friends, after all, weren't they? Sure, she wasn't as close with him as she was with his sister, but still...

Marilyn wasn't sure what she would feel the next time she saw him. Betrayal? Curiosity? Amusement? Maybe all of the above.

She wondered if Hannah knew. It would hurt a lot if Nate had never told his sister.

She picked up her phone and texted:

*Give me a call when you're on break*

She sent it off to Hannah.

\*

Hannah didn't see Marilyn's text until she was heading away from the front desk for her break. It had been a riotous morning at the clinic, and for that she was grateful. What with the various surgeries coming in first thing in the morning, the emergencies (How *did* that Siamese manage to get the peanut butter jar stuck on its head in the first place?), and the usual complement of nail clippings, vaccinations, and checkups, Hannah had hardly had a chance to catch her breath, let alone think about the mess she had created for her brother.

Now, as she sat in the break room with an orange and her smartphone, she wondered what Marilyn could want to talk to her about. She was off on Monday and Sunday, and usually, Hannah didn't hear from her on those days. The normally gregarious woman disappeared on her "weekends," holing up in her apartment with a virtual stack of new e-books, boxes of Fran's chocolates, and a Pandora station tuned to the new-age wonders of a station called Spa. In other words, Marilyn treasured her alone time.

So Hannah was concerned that she had reached out to her. She called her friend immediately.

"Hi, hon, what's up?" Hannah asked as soon as Marilyn answered.

"Did you know about your brother?" Marilyn asked.

Hannah immediately panicked. Had Nate been hurt? Had Marilyn somehow found out about what had happened with Brandon and OpenHeartOpenMind? "I'm not sure what you mean."

"You didn't know, did you? Because I would think if you knew, you'd get my reference right off the bat, especially with all the shit going around on Facebook about it."

Hannah shook her head, feeling her eyebrows inch toward one another in confusion. What had Nate done now? In spite of the problems resulting from her Whos2Know profile, Hannah couldn't begin to imagine what her friend was talking about.

"I still don't get you." Hannah glanced down at her watch. Her break was only fifteen minutes. If Marilyn didn't get to the point soon, she would be out of time. She didn't think she could stand going back to work with the suspense of unanswered questions hanging over her. "Spit it out. I don't have much more time."

"You know that author I told you about, BF Mann?"

"Yeah..." Hannah wasn't sure where this was going. The question seemed like a non sequitur.

"Well, you know who she—excuse me, he—is, don't you?"

Hannah sighed, frustrated. Had Marilyn already been hitting the Bloody Marys this morning? Because this conversation was making no sense at all. "You mentioned the books and that I should read them. I haven't had a chance yet." Hannah glanced down at her watch again. She cradled the phone between her ear and shoulder as she emptied her orange peels into the trash. "Listen, I have to be getting back to work. I don't mean to be rude, but what's your point, sweetheart?"

"BF Mann is your brother."

Hannah sat back down. Had she heard right? Or had she said BF Mann is your *mother*? Or *brother from another planet*? She giggled. "What?"

"You heard me. You really didn't know?"

"Wait. You're telling me my brother is an author? And he writes gay romance?" Many puzzle pieces fell into place now, particularly the ones about how Nate made his living. She was more surprised her brother had been able to keep such a secret under her nose for the past several years. She had just taken at face value his story that he was doing underwriting reports for a living. But who did that, anyway?

Who made a living as a gay romance author?

Her brother, apparently. Hannah felt a hot mix of emotions course through her—pride with confusion, excitement with doubt. In the end, Hannah felt a little hurt that her brother had kept this from her, but dumbfounded in a good way that he had managed to make a living as a real living and breathing author.

She had so many questions to ask him! She wished she could run right home and ask them all now. But Hannah lived in the real world. She was not her own boss (as authors were) and couldn't just slip out of a busy workplace because she was preoccupied with questions. No, she would have to keep her head down, stay focused, and work out the remaining hours of her shift, no matter how burning her need to know.

"My break's over. I gotta go." Hannah stood and then sat down again. Hard. "Wait a minute! You're pulling my leg, you bitch!" Hannah laughed, recalling that, a while back, Marilyn had showed her this BF Mann person's website, complete with the woman's picture. Hannah couldn't recall much about what the woman looked like, but she was sure BF Mann was a woman. And if BF Mann had been her brother, wouldn't she have recognized him? "You showed me the website, Marilyn. BF Mann is a woman, a middle-aged woman. I remember. Is this your way of punking me?"

"Take a look at the website now." Marilyn blurted out the URL, and Hannah, in spite of the fact that her break was now over and she was preventing someone else on the front desk from having a few minutes of peace, brought out her smartphone and typed in the URL.

"Oh my God." Hannah stared at the picture of her baby brother and, for a moment, believed the world had shifted, tilted a little. She skimmed the "coming clean" blog post and sucked in a big breath.

"So what do you think?" Marilyn asked. "Any idea what the little shit had up his sleeve?"

"Nope. None. Nate doesn't even like to read." Hannah stared down at the BF Mann website in wonder. "Or so I thought." She made herself stand again when she heard the door to the break room creak open. Chanel Waters, the next person up for a break, glared at Hannah from behind her horn-rims.

"Listen, Marilyn. I gotta go. I'll call you later." She snapped the phone shut and gave what she hoped was an appropriately sheepish grin to her coworker.

She edged by Chanel, having no idea how she'd make it through the day. Nate was a novelist? A gay romance novelist?

Since when? Hannah giggled again, but there was little mirth in it.

With whom was she living, anyway?

And hey! Who was he to be getting all self-righteous about her pretending to be someone else?

# Chapter Seventeen

When his phone rang and Nate's face came up on the screen, Brandon decided he had treated the guy to enough silence. He grinned and pressed the screen to accept the call.

"Hey."

"Hey, you. Listen, I'm really sorry about everything."

"It's okay. Your sister wrote me."

"I know. She told me. I'm sorry about that too. She said you deleted your account over it."

Brandon laughed, pushing the plastic container that had held his lunchtime fish and chips away. He held the phone between shoulder and ear while he wiped his fingers on a paper napkin. "That wasn't why I deleted my account."

"It wasn't?" Brandon could detect a note of relief in Nate's voice.

"No. I just was through with that site. I think I've had enough with meeting people online." He took a sip of his vitamin water and set it back down on the Formica-topped table of the little dive he had gone to for lunch that day. "Especially when I have met the one I wanted to meet all along." Brandon was sure the smile he punctuated that statement with headed through the phone, even if Nate couldn't see it. The smile was broad enough, Brandon thought, to be felt.

Nate said, "Aw, man, it's so good to hear you say that."

"Wait a minute. Who said it was you?"

Nate sounded flustered as he said, "I just assumed. I'm sorry..."

Brandon laughed. "Of course it's you, dummy. I haven't dated anyone else in months." He picked up the detritus from his lunch and deposited it in a wastebasket and headed outside, where the warm breeze could caress him until he had to head back into the office high-rise. "But seriously, I feel I got a little burned on that whole deal. I just thought, Nate, if we're going to move forward, if we're going to have any chance at all, we have to be honest." Brandon was sure Nate agreed, which is why he was surprised by the silence that extended for several seconds on the other end of the call.

"Nate? You still there?"

"Yeah, yeah, sure!" Nate didn't say anything for a while again. "I was just fixing myself some lunch. Sorry, preoccupied."

"It's okay. Listen, do you want to come over for dinner tonight? I put some chicken breasts in the fridge to thaw this morning and thought I'd do a stir-fry. I make a great peanut sauce. Maybe we could fit in a run before and—"

"I'd love to," Nate said.

"You would? Good! Good. I'll see you at around seven?"

"Perfect. I'll bring a bottle of Pinot Grigio."

*

When they hung up, Nate realized the wine might be necessary after he told Brandon the truth about his real occupation. He hadn't expected the fallout to be as big as it was, but within minutes of posting his blog, his readers were already chattering away about it on Facebook, Twitter, and the m/m romance author loops. It was as though his using a pen name had offended many of them personally.

He could kind of get it, he thought, sitting down out on the back patio of their town house with a bottle of water and a tuna salad sandwich. It was impossible to work today, with all the anxiety he was experiencing. Those readers, though, who felt like he had "slapped them in the face," had a point only in that maybe he had crossed a line when he posted pictures of "himself," or "herself," not only on his website but across several social media platforms as well.

They felt deceived, as though they had made virtual friends with someone who had been hiding behind a mask the whole time when they, in fact, had not.

Nate shook his head, thinking of the many Facebook posts and emails readers had sent Ms. Mann over the years. They had bared their personal lives and made themselves vulnerable, while he answered them in character, throwing in unnecessary lies about "her" life in San Diego, "her" husband, Drake, and their four beautiful children, little Ashley finally gone off to college at UCLA. Sniff, sniff.

That much, Nate decided with embarrassment and shame, had been wrong. *You don't let a friend believe you are someone else, even if the friend is only an online acquaintance.* He realized he needed to write another blog, one of apology to his readers, and reveal that it was never his intention to hurt.

He had never intended for things to spiral so out of control when he picked the pen name. In another age, when things weren't so instantly available online, there wouldn't have been the temptation to connect so personally with readers. But one thing had led to another, and soon Nate had created an entire life for BF Mann. It had been fun, imagining all the things she was up to and her quirky personality. She had become like a character in one of his novels.

He could have kicked himself for never realizing the stock people might come to put in this woman, this writer whom they adored.

Until this morning...

Pen names were one thing. And Nate still didn't believe he had done anything wrong by adopting one. Writers had been doing that much since time immemorial.

He realized what he had done wasn't so very different from what his sister and Marilyn had done, and it had spiraled out of control in much the same way (although his had much bigger consequences). He understood now what had happened, how an online persona could be fun, how we could create a whole new person to be.

Who among us hasn't longed to be someone else, if only for a day?

Nate got up. He wasn't enjoying the warm, balmy breezes, wasn't able to eat more than a few bites of his sandwich.

He needed to talk to his readers. He trudged back up to the third floor, sat at his desk, and opened his laptop.

He opened a new blog post and stared at the empty screen. And then he began to type.

*Dear Reader,*

*I am writing just to you, the one who has been hurt by my admission earlier today that BF Mann is not a woman but a gay man. I wanted to apologize, to tell you how deeply I regret letting things get out of hand. I never meant to hurt you. In fact, if I could go back and do things differently, I would. Because I love all of you; I have loved communicating with you, even if I was foolishly hiding behind a mask.*

*I hope I haven't damaged things beyond all repair. And I don't say that because I am worried about sales, or that you will turn away from my next offering, but because one of the greatest treasures I believe any writer has is his or her connection to a reader. A reader like you. It might be on the page, when together, with my words and your imagination, we build a story. Or it might be on Facebook, exchanging messages and good-natured snark. Authors work in an isolated place, and believe me when I say I treasure my connection to you. I would be inconsolable if I thought my actions had done anything to permanently damage that.*

*It started with a pen name, and that was all I ever intended it to be. Like the characters in my books, BF Mann took on a life of her own. She's a wild woman and got a little out of control.*

*I had to rein her in. I had to tell you the truth. I apologize many times over for deceiving you, but malice was never in my heart. Know I never snickered at you or thought you were foolish for believing in my persona. As I said, I treasured that interaction, and it never even crossed my mind that I could be doing you harm.*

*I hope you can find it in your heart to forgive me. I have many more stories to tell, both personal and the kind you like—juicy gay love stories spiced with the paranormal or a big dose of suspense, all set right here where I do live (honest!), in Seattle.*

*For me—and I suspect for you too—it's always been about the stories and not as much the person behind them. I know I will remember that going forward and hope you will as well.*

*I heart you.*

*Nate*


He hoped the blog wasn't too much and that it didn't come off as insincere. He prayed, with all his heart, that his readers, his beloved readers, saw that he was baring his soul along with the real him, and in that act, dreamed of a kind of grace—or at least forgiveness.

He hit Publish.

*

Brandon left work early. Now that his anger at being deceived by Nate's sister (and yes, by extension, Nate too) had ebbed, he was at last eager to get back to the point where they had been before the fallout—two young guys who might be falling for one another.

Thus the reason for leaving work early. He stopped on his way home at a drugstore and picked up a fresh bottle of lube and a dozen condoms. (Not that he thought they would need them *all* tonight, but a girl could dream!)

He wandered by Pike Place Market and picked up a bouquet of beautiful fresh wildflowers.

At home, he put clean sheets on the bed and trimmed the wicks of all the candles Nate had bought in his sadly aborted attempt at romance from just a few days ago. He made sure he had matches to light them.

He put fresh soap in the shower and had gotten a toothbrush for Nate too.

And then he realized, after all this, he had forgotten to stop at Whole Foods to pick up the broccoli he had planned on using to make their dinner. "You are such a dizzy queen!" he scolded himself, laughing. "Too excited at the prospect of getting some cock."

Brandon shrugged. They could order pizza. He had a feeling they would be consuming dessert first, anyway. He pulled back the covers on the bed, smoothed the sheets, and fluffed the pillows.

He ducked into the shower, questioning if he wanted to wait, since he had mentioned going for a run with Nate, but then thought the hell with *that*. There were much better ways to amp up the heart rate and to start the sweat flowing.

Amazing, Brandon thought, stepping out of the shower and drying himself off, how a little drama being resolved could light a fire to the tinderbox of desire. He turned in front of the partially steamed mirror, admiring his work in the shower. He had shaved the hair from above his cock, on his balls, and the sensitive area between there and his asshole. His body looked firm, taut, ready for anything—and his cock suddenly appeared to be a lot bigger. It was all about illusion.

Should he answer the door naked?

He recalled coming home and finding Nate in bed the other day and how that attempt at romance had ended in disaster. Maybe it was time for a do-over. What did they call it in the game of golf? A mulligan?

So Brandon remained undressed and half hard as he took the daisies from the bouquet of flowers he had purchased from the market and scattered their petals in a trail leading up to his bed. He wished he had red roses as Nate had, but it was a little late for that now.

He glanced at the clock and saw that it was almost seven. He went to the bedroom to lie down in what he hoped was a provocative pose, at least if "provocative" could be described as legs spread and an almost painful erection rising up out of a mat of dark pubic hair.

He had a sneaking suspicion that most of his gay brethren would be on the same page with him about the meaning of provocative.

Just as he was admiring the glistening, blood-engorged head of his cock, the phone rang. "This better not be you, Nate. I swear to God, if you're late, I may have to take matters into my own hands." He laughed and reached for the phone.

His mom, Nancy. Brandon rolled his eyes, thinking how weird it would be talking to his mother in his current state of dishabille and arousal. But—as he had never hidden from anyone—he was a mama's boy through and through. And mama's boys, no matter what was going on, did not ignore calls from their mothers.

What if something was wrong?

He pulled the sheet up over his junk and pressed the screen to answer. "Hey, Nancy."

"What's up, son?"

*Oh Lord, this is like a bad sitcom.* Brandon stared down at the tent his hard-on had made under the sheet. "Just waiting for my date to show up."

"Nate? He was charming. I wasn't too sure about this online dating thing, but after meeting him, I think you got lucky."

*And I am hoping to get lucky in a few minutes, here. That is, if a nice chat with my mother isn't a total thrill kill.* His cock was slowly deflating with the sound of Nancy's voice.

"Yeah. We hit a little snag, but things are much better now. I really have high hopes for this one, Nancy."

"That's good to hear." His mom, for once, went quiet for several moments. Usually, when her tongue stopped wagging, it meant she was preparing to say something momentous.

"What?"

"Nothing! Nothing!" Nancy's voice went higher, and Brandon knew his mom's bravado was for show.

"Did you call for a reason? Not to be rude, but he's going to be here any second now, and I'm really excited to see him." *I was more excited before your ill-timed phone call, but I'm sure we can get right back to where we started. It's all right.* "As I said, we had a tiny bit of drama, and now we're ready to make up." *Oh God, did I just say that? To my mother?* "I think tonight will be a very special date."

Nancy was quiet once more.

"Mom? Is there something on your mind?"

She didn't answer. Finally, she said, "No, nothing. But before I let you go, just let me ask you this: Are you sure you know Nate as well as you think you do?"

"That's an odd question."

"Like, for example, do you know what he does for a living?"

Brandon chuckled. "Don't worry, Nancy, he's gainfully employed. A good prospect—I'm just about to reel him in. He'll keep me, I'm sure, at least in the manner to which I've become accustomed."

"That wasn't what I meant."

"What did you mean?"

"Nothing. Just ask him about his work." Nancy sighed. "A man's work helps define him, don't you think?"

"What are you talking about?"

"It's not important. We'll chat later—like tomorrow. I'm not so old that I would forget and call you later tonight. If I must get in touch, I'll text. That way you can ignore me." She laughed. "Have fun."

"I intend to."

He hung up. And another call came in. Ah, blessed relief. The caller ID said, simply, Intercom.

He knew who was knocking at his door, so he pressed the button on his phone's keypad that would admit Nate.

"Shit," he whispered and raced to the front door, unlocked it, and left it open just a crack. He hurried back to the bed, where he flung the sheets back and flung himself down atop them, legs splayed.

He was hard once more.

He listened as Nate came into the apartment, his subtle footfall on the bamboo flooring. He heard the rustle of clothes and realized this was all too perfect. Nate had gotten the right idea; he was undressing.

Brandon only had one panicked moment as he thought that perhaps someone else had come to call. Maybe the building's maintenance man would come walking into his bedroom to find Brandon wearing nothing but a smile. Or his horndog buddy, Christian, whom he hadn't seen in quite a while. Christian, he was afraid, would be straddling him before he had a chance to get a word out, sliding down on his cock bareback before Brandon had had time to draw breath, let alone protest.

Christian was just that way, especially when faced with the prospect of raw man meat.

But life, apparently, was finished with tossing Brandon wild cards, at least for the moment, because it was Nate who entered the room.

Naked Nate, smiling. Their eyes met, and Brandon knew there was no need for words. He realized his own passion, plain enough by the hard-on rising up between his muscled thighs, was also written on his face. His lips were moist and parted, eyes sparkling with desire.

He saw the same reflected in Nate. Beautiful Nate. The late afternoon sun slanted into the room perfectly to illuminate the ice blue of his eyes, and a wave of lust washed over Brandon, practically blocking out all conscious thought. He took it all in—the broad shoulders and firm pecs that made a kind of shelf across Nate's chest, dotted with alert, delicious-looking reddish-brown nipples. A thin line of peach fuzz pointed downward, like neon, to his cock, which matched Brandon's in its state of arousal. His legs were like tree trunks, defined, poised to spring, and made firm and taut from years of running.

*He is simply the most perfect specimen of manhood who has ever stood in this bedroom*, Brandon thought. And the most wondrous thing was not his looks, which were stellar and swoon inducing, but the glow in his eyes and the smile on his face, which conveyed not only lust, but also something more important—kindness.

Brandon became a vessel of need, holding his arms out hungrily. Nate moved toward him, a little awkward, his hard-on bobbing before him like a baton, ready to orchestrate their connection.

Nate slid onto the bed beside Brandon and, wordlessly, took him into his arms. Nate's mouth was that of a starving man's as he kissed him, his lips meeting Brandon's in a frenzy, his tongue darting inside Brandon's mouth to explore the hot cave. Brandon sucked the tongue hungrily, biting down gently, opening his eyes to meet the blurry blue of Nate's own.

They pulled against each other, arms needy, their bodies meshing together hard—as though they wanted to make two one.

And indeed, they did.

Like a blanket of silken skin, Nate covered Brandon, moving his kisses from his mouth to his eyelids, to his neck, to the ticklishness of his ears. He paused for a moment, and Brandon stared up at him, breathless with lust and anticipation.

To Brandon it looked as though Nate was contemplating what to do next. Brandon didn't care what it was, as long as it was *something*. His nerve endings felt electrified with need. There was a fiery hunger in his belly that could only be satisfied by the warmth of real connection.

Finally, Nate got himself up into a straddling position atop Brandon and reached back to grip the steel of Brandon's cock. He poised himself above it, ready to slide down.

Every impulse in Brandon told him to go ahead and let Nate do it—that warmth, that silken glove he anticipated surrounding his cock was heaven within a hairbreadth's reach. Worry about safety and common sense later, he told himself. The body wants what it wants, needs what it needs.

But a tiny amount of self-preservation survived the carnal onslaught, and, breathlessly, he whispered, "Whoa there, sweetheart."

Nate's hungry eyes engaged with Brandon's own.

"Rubbers and lube are on the nightstand."

Quickly, almost so fast it seemed like magic, Nate had Brandon's pulsing cock sheathed in latex and slicked up with lube. Grinning, he poured a dollop of the slippery stuff onto his fingertips and smeared his asshole.

"Got any poppers?" Nate wondered. "You're so modest you probably don't even realize how big you are." He glanced over his shoulder and returned his gaze to Brandon, grinning. "Or thick."

Brandon smiled and shook his head. "Just go slow."

But apparently Nate was too hungry, too intent to have Brandon inside him, to follow Brandon's simple directive. He slid down almost savagely on Brandon's cock, taking him inside with one fell swoop.

It was incredible. Brandon was certain that, for just one second, his heart stopped beating and his respiration ceased as his cock was engulfed in a hot, tight dampness—perfect. It was like an oiled hand gripping him tightly.

He could have screamed.

He could have passed out.

Instead, he simply whispered, "Do not move." Because he knew if Nate made the tiniest attempt to begin bouncing up and down on his cock, he would shoot immediately. It felt that good. *God, just give me a moment for things to calm down, for my cock to stop throbbing, just seconds shy of exploding.*

They stared into one another's eyes, playing a waiting game. Brandon could feel the pulse of his cock blessedly begin to ease up. His muscles began to relax, and at last he pushed upward, more deeply into Nate.

They both made a sound in unison—a cross between a groan and a sigh.

And then Nate began moving slowly, riding Brandon. The pace was almost leisurely at first, but as their passion stoked, so did the tempo, and Nate began moving faster and faster, taking his pleasure like a starving vessel. Their small cries mirrored the ecstasy their bodies fed them. They began to sweat, and Brandon, unable to lie still, began to thrust upward to match Nate's downward pushes.

"Fuck," Brandon whispered, sitting up and pushing on Nate's chest. Nate went over backward, his legs in the air. Brandon grabbed the muscular calves, flung them over his shoulders, and shoved the entire length of himself into Nate. Hard.

Nate did not complain but wriggled down on the cock to get Brandon inside him even farther.

The fucking reached a frenzied crescendo, faster and faster, Brandon's hips a blur as he pounded into Nate, the box springs squeaking and the headboard banging against the wall. Their cries were loud, primal.

In the moment just before he came, Brandon thought that people on the street below could probably hear all this through his open window.

He didn't care. "Fuck. I'm gonna come!" he yelled, burying himself with one final, savage thrust.

"Fill me up, baby. I want that load in me." Nate held onto Brandon's ass as he bucked and writhed, emptying himself. Then Nate pushed him back just a little, so their chests separated. "Look what you do to me," he gasped as white jets of spunk shot out of him, without so much as his touch. The come landed first on Nate's cheek, then his chin, and worked its way in a line down his throat, chest, and at last, his belly.

Brandon reached down with his tongue to lick the largest dollops away from Nate's cheek and chin—and then kissed him deeply, swirling the come around in their mouths until Nate swallowed it greedily.

At last, Brandon collapsed atop Nate's body, panting.

After a long while, Brandon's breathing, as did Nate's, returned to a semblance of normal, and his heart rate moved from heart attack stage to simply pounding. He moved off of Nate but held him close, their skin sealed together with sweat, come, and spit.

"Was that everything you hoped it would be?" Nate wondered.

"It was good," Brandon said, a little breathless, "but I've had better."

Nate punched him, and they laughed. "Seriously," Brandon said, "that was amazing." And it had been. Brandon simply didn't know if words were enough to encompass what he felt at this moment. Physically, the sex was incredible, beyond his wildest hopes, but there was something else, too, a sense of connection, of shared humanity that continued to grow in the afterglow. This was a feeling Brandon thought could only be described as love, although he wondered if it would be wrong to say the words.

*Isn't it awful we live in a world where we question a desire to tell another person we love them? That we worry that it's too soon or what motivates it? Well, I am not going to think that way.*

"I love you," he whispered quickly, shyly, in Nate's ear, hoping he wasn't ruining this magical mood. He knew in his heart that this was more than just the aftereffects of mind-blowing sex.

Nate's hug, fierce, breath withheld, told Brandon all he needed to know as a response, yet Nate whispered, "Me too."

They lay in silence for a long while, a cool breeze that foretold fall causing them to cling to one another. It was this clinging that precipitated a second round, this time slower and more tender.

When that was done, Brandon at last said the words men the world over uttered *most* often, straight or gay—"I'm hungry."

Nate sat up next to him. "You said you were going to make dinner."

Brandon smiled sadly. "I was all caught up in getting ready for *this*, and I totally forgot to stop and get everything I needed. I hope that's okay. We could order a pizza."

Nate swung his legs over the side of the bed. "Before you reach for the phone, let me go nose around your kitchen."

"Okay. I'll help." Brandon started to get up, but Nate pushed him back down on the bed and kissed the tip of his nose. "You just stay there. If we need to call in reinforcements, we can do that. But I'm a pretty good cook and a *very* good improviser, so you just lie back and rest. I *did* wear you out, didn't I? If you say no, this was an epic fail."

"Oh, you wore me out all right. I think my dick has rug burns."

"I'll kiss it better later." Nate hopped from the bed and stooped down to grab his boxers. He slid into them.

"I could get used to this," Brandon said, bunching a pillow up under his head.

"Not too. Next time for sure is your turn."

"Deal."

\*

In the kitchen, Nate started by looking through the cupboards. He could not stop grinning, and he felt like his face had been painted in an expression of delight and contentment so entrenched that he would never be able to do anything again other than smile. If he could whistle, he would have done so. He was in that kind of mood.

He found a box of pasta, a jar of crunchy peanut butter, and a box of chicken stock. "Perfect," he whispered, setting the trio out on the counter. He moved to the refrigerator, where he moved stuff around, hoping he'd find some chicken or maybe tofu. Sure enough, there were two boneless, skinless chicken breasts, already thawed. He pulled them out and went back in, this time raiding the crisper, where he found a red pepper, some scallions, and even a bag of already cleaned and washed snow peas.

He got the water boiling for the vermicelli and set a sauté pan on the stove heating with a dollop of peanut oil and a few drops of dark sesame oil. Immediately, the kitchen smelled amazing.

He went to the refrigerator one more time, hoping. "God bless you," he whispered when he found a bottle of Tamari soy sauce, some Sriracha, and even a hunk of fresh ginger.

"This dinner is meant to be." He got busy chopping, and soon he was throwing the meal together—hunks of chicken breast with vermicelli, scallions, and red pepper, coated with a lovely peanut sauce. It smelled wonderful, and, although he could do a lot better, he thought it was a pretty good attempt for just grabbing odds and ends out of the kitchen. He dished the pasta up in deep bowls and then looked for chopsticks, sesame seeds, or peanuts in Brandon's cupboard, but found none.

"Can't have everything." He chopped a few green onion tops to use as a garnish, then loaded it all on a tray.

The romantic idea would have been to serve Brandon dinner in bed. But he paused as he headed in that direction, thinking of the sweat- and come-soaked sheets, the delicious smell of sex lingering in the air. Appetizing, yes—for more sex. But for food? Not so much.

He glanced around him, then positioned the coffee table near the sliding glass doors, now open to the night breeze. The wind brought in the smell of grass, leaves, and the fishy tang of the lake just a few hundred yards over. Twilight had just about completed the sky's transformation into full-on night, yet there was a lovely line of lavender at the horizon.

Nate set dinner up on the table, throwing a couple of pillows from the couch onto the floor. As a finishing touch, he lit a candle and set its flickering warmth as a centerpiece.

He hurried into the bedroom, where he was surprised—and kind of touched—to find Brandon asleep. Again, he thought of how a romantic vision clashed with reality. If he were writing this scene, Nate thought his main character would find his lover asleep and cock his head in awe and wonder at how much the slumberer looked like a child—innocent and in contented repose. The reality, though, was that Brandon lay on his back, one arm flung over his head, his mouth open in a window-shaking snore. A line of drool had run down his cheek.

Nate laughed, and his chuckle caused Brandon to stir. His eyes fluttered open. He sucked in a breath and got himself up on his elbows. "Sorry. I guess if your aim was to wear me out, you succeeded."

"You want to sleep a little more? I made dinner, but it'll be just as good cold—peanut noodles."

"No, no. I'm starved."

Nate reached down and plucked a T-shirt and boxers off the floor and threw them to Brandon. "The air coming in through the sliding glass doors is a little chilly. Otherwise I'd want to eat naked." He winked. "Then eat *you* naked."

Nate took Brandon's hand. "Come on."

Brandon smiled at Nate as he took in the set table. "You did this for me?"

"It's nothin'. Let's eat."

*

After dinner, Brandon suggested they take a walk. "We both smell like sex and sweat."

"And the problem with that is?"

"Ah, I just want to get it blown off of us before we begin the next round. A little walk down by the lakefront? I know a pier that hardly anyone uses, especially at night. We can sit out on the water for a bit."

"Sounds nice."

Brandon picked up the dishes from the table and took them into the kitchen. "I'll clean up later. Whoever cooks does not have to clean up. That's the first rule."

"What's the second?"

"Sex every night." Brandon grinned and hurried into the kitchen.

"Those sound like rules I can live by, even if I am a bit of a rebel," Nate called from the living room. Brandon could hear the rustle of his getting dressed.

They walked hand in hand down Green Lake Way, the quiet evening surrounding them. Brandon felt something he hoped Nate did too—contentment and a kind of wonder as well, that they had found themselves here so soon.

But when it was right, it was right. Right?

The solitude and bliss was cut into by the sound of Brandon's phone, alerting him that he had a text. He pulled the phone from a pocket in his cargo shorts and saw the message from his mom.

"Check this out," she had written. This was followed by blue text, a URL for a website, BFMann.com, and then, "Did he tell you yet?"

Brandon stared down at the screen, feeling the confusion twist his features.

"What is it?" Nate asked, slowing.

Brandon handed him the phone and watched Nate's face as it clouded over with concern, the ease of the past few minutes replaced by a frown. Nate pressed down the button on top of the phone, holding it. He slid his finger across the screen, and Brandon knew he had switched it off. "We don't need interruptions right now, right?" He handed the phone back to Brandon, smiling.

Brandon took it, puzzled and concerned. He easily read Nate's smile as falsely bright. He shrugged and tucked the phone back into his pocket. "The pier's right over here. Let's cross."

They waited for a break in the traffic and then dashed across the street.

They sat at the edge of the pier, the only ones occupying it, their legs dangling above the water.

The pier was near the end of Sixty-fifth, in a part of the park far from the beaches, aqua theater, and other more populated places of the lakefront. It jutted out into the lake, which was now almost silent—a shimmery darkness at their feet. Wind rustled the leaves in the trees. Across the water, dimly, they saw a couple of men with a lantern, casting fishing lines.

"This is nice, isn't it?" Brandon slid his arm around Nate's shoulder and drew him close.

\*

Nate leaned into Brandon, wishing the moment hadn't been spoiled by Brandon's mom's text. He knew he'd have to tell Brandon the truth about his occupation sooner rather than later, with the social media buzz now surrounding it, but he was hoping it would not be tonight when things were going so perfectly.

Life and its damned timing!

The text had set Nate's nerves on end, making it hard to relax. He could feel himself grinding his teeth and forced himself to stop. How would he tell Brandon? And worse, would Brandon see it as yet another deception? Coming so close on the heels of what Hannah (and he) had pulled, he didn't know where this would put them.

"You're awfully quiet. You seem a thousand miles away," Brandon said, and Nate realized Brandon was staring at him.

"Sorry." Nate still didn't move his gaze from the water. It had always been his belief, mantra maybe, to live his life without regrets, yet at the moment he wished he could go back and change everything, including his ill-considered literary decision to present himself to the world as a middle-aged straight woman.

But do-overs did not happen in real life. Marilyn would have said, "You made your bed, now fuck in it." He could actually hear her in his head. He hoped there would still be some fucking for him and Brandon after he dropped his news. He hoped there would still be *something*, that his revelation wouldn't be like a superbomb, vaporizing everything.

Nate knew it was unfair, but he turned more toward Brandon and asked, "Is there anything I could say that would make you hate me?"

Brandon's face clouded over with concern and confusion. "Hate you?" He shook his head. "I don't think so. Why, are you a serial killer? Cheat on your taxes? Wear white after Labor Day? Have a drug habit?"

"No, none of those." Nate stared out at the water and drew in a deep breath. "Remember when I told you what I did for a living?"

"Uh-huh."

"Well, that wasn't quite true. I do write for a living, but not underwriting reports as I said. I was kind of on the down low about what I actually wrote, God only knows why now." He sighed.

And he felt Brandon, very subtly, stiffen beside him.

"On the down low?" Brandon asked.

Nate nodded. He couldn't look at Brandon. "Look. It's no big deal. I write gay romance, and I do pretty well at it. That text your mom sent you? That was to my website." He forced himself to meet Brandon's eyes, already hating the hurt he could see reflected there.

"I am BF Mann."

"I thought BF Mann was a woman."

"Do I look like a woman? Don't answer that." Nate told Brandon all about how the genre, to him, seemed to embrace female writers and how he and his publisher, once upon a time, had made the decision to adopt a gender-neutral name and to put him out there as a she. "It was stupid, I know. It should be just about the stories, right? Not whether I had a penis or a vagina." He felt Brandon's arm slip from around his shoulders, and cold, both literal and figurative, rushed in to replace its absence. "Things just sort of took on a life of their own. It's crazy today, with Facebook and Twitter and all those other sites. There's no distance now between a writer and his public. They want to know. And once I started lying, I couldn't stop."

Nate felt a queasiness rise up in his gut. He hoped he could ameliorate the word "lying" by saying, "But, as of this morning, I came clean to my readers and the world in general—on my website. I even posted a picture of myself." He tried to engage Brandon's gaze, but Brandon wouldn't look back at him, which hurt. "I did it after what happened with OpenHeartOpenMind. I hated that our relationship was born in deceit. I just wanted to get all the deceit out of my life."

"And so now you're telling me you lied about who you were to your readers and lied to me about what you did for a living." Brandon paused, considering. Then he sat up straighter, as though something had just occurred to him. "You even lied to Nancy, my mom. She was gabbing away the other night at dinner about BF Mann, and you didn't give away a thing, did you?" He didn't wait for a reply but laughed—bitterly. "I do have to hand it to you. You have a wonderful poker face." He stood up, brushing at the back of his shorts.

"Sit down, Brandon."

"No. No, I'm gonna go home."

Nate looked up at him, feeling the hot prick of tears in his eyes. "Can I come?"

Brandon squatted down next to him. He ran his fingers through Nate's hair. "No." He pulled his hand away. "Do you remember my ad on that site? One of the words I used was honest. That's important to me. Now, I get that what happened with the site wasn't really your fault, and what you're telling me now is all about some boneheaded career move in an arena I know nothing about, so maybe being someone else was the right choice.

"But I'm too simple, too uncomplicated to want that in my life. I want a guy who is who he says he is. It's hard to turn away from you, sweetheart, it really is. You're a gorgeous guy—and I do feel something for you beyond just the physical, although I have to admit, that's pretty hot. But there are too many red flags here, and they tripped my fight-or-flee meter. Because it's still way early days with us, I think it's best I cut my losses and move on, tempting as it is to stay."

Brandon shrugged and finally stood again. "I can't do this. I just don't know that I could trust you. And without trust, there's nothing."

Nate waited for him to say more, but all Brandon did was turn and walk away. Nate watched him as he grew dimmer and more indistinct, fading into the shadows. A strong impulse told him to run after Brandon, to try to explain how, at heart, he really wasn't a dishonest person. But he stayed rooted to his spot on the pier, knowing there was nothing he could say to make things better.

He returned to gazing out at the water. The dark surface mirrored how he felt.

*

Brandon made it two blocks before he started crying. Before that, he was grim, not thinking, his lips drawn in a taut line across his face. "Damn it," he scolded himself, wiping the tears angrily away. "He's not worth it. And you should not act like such a baby."

A dark-haired man walking a Boston terrier turned the corner and eyed Brandon suspiciously. The dog barked.

"Oh, what are you two doing out this late? Or early? Or whatever?" Brandon called over his shoulder, hurrying on.

The dog barked again.

He stopped for a moment by a Peet's Coffee and leaned against its brick façade to compose himself. It was silly, he tried to reason, to be upset. He was doing the right thing. Nancy would agree. Hell, the world would agree. You don't build a relationship on such a shaky foundation. And when you're lucky enough to find out so early on, it shouldn't be such a big deal to let go.

Yet it was.

There was something in what he felt for Nate that defied logic. There was a connection there born of more than simple lust and attraction, a feeling they belonged together, that a future, with the proper nurturing, could take root and bloom.

*Don't do this to yourself. You know they made up that saying about plenty more fish in the sea for a reason. You are young and reasonably smart and attractive. Put yourself out there. There's a nice—and honest—guy somewhere just waiting for you. And he doesn't have all the baggage. When you eventually find him and you wake up next to him, you won't wonder who you're waking up beside, because there will be only one of him.*

*With Nate, you'll never know for sure. Is it BF Mann lying beside you? Hannah Tippie? Nate himself? Some other version of the man?*

*No, this is not a way to start a relationship, not with mistrust and deceit, however innocent it is or devoid of malice.*

*Let go. Move on. In a few weeks, you'll look back at this episode and know you did the right thing.*

Brandon started walking again, his footfalls echoing in the silence. Something about that last thought rankled him, and it was these words: in a few weeks. He considered those few weeks—bleak, empty, alone, no Nate to make him smile, to feed his various hungers, to keep life interesting.

Yes, even though they had only just met, the man had managed to make significant inroads into Brandon's heart, and Brandon didn't know how easy it would be to block off those entrances, to fill them in with emotional concrete.

He neared his apartment and wondered what it would make of him if he were successful in hardening his heart toward Nate. Would it make him smarter? Better? Less vulnerable?

And were any of those things worth losing the man with whom he was falling in love? Nate was the first man in a long time who had stirred such feelings within him.

Brandon shook his head as he neared the front of his apartment building. He was suddenly washed over with weariness and didn't think he could debate himself any longer. The emotional drain (and the sexual one too) had taken everything out of him, and the fatigue caught up all at once.

He had sick days at work. He would take one tomorrow. Right now, nothing seemed more appealing than crawling into bed and sleeping for ten or twelve hours, hoping his life—the mess, joy, and despair of it—would all seem better in the morning, under a summer sun.

He took out his keys and headed inside. He paused for a moment to turn his phone back on, but promised himself he wouldn't look at it—not for a long while. Sleep first.

*

Brandon's phone rang, lifting him up from a deep, dreamless sleep that, upon waking, felt more like a coma than slumber. He looked down at the illuminated screen and saw the word *Intercom*. Glancing at the top of the screen, he saw it was a little after 5:00 a.m.

He didn't know who could be coming to call at five in the morning and was tempted to ignore it. Fortunately, he had a view of the front door from his balcony. Phone in hand, he stepped outside.

Peering through the wan light of early morning, he saw him: Nate. It took a moment, Brandon supposed, for him to realize Brandon was looking down at him, and then he must have sensed it, for he looked up at Brandon, their eyes meeting through the watery grayish light. Even from his vantage point on the balcony, Brandon could detect a plaintive sadness in Nate's eyes, and it caused his heart to clench.

Once again, his head and heart were at war. His head told him to go back inside, close the glass door to the balcony, and shut off his phone. He could lie in bed—alone—and feel self-righteous. At least *he* was honest.

But his heart nudged him in another direction, as his head knew it would. Brandon, after all, was above all else, a romantic.

"What are you doing?" he whispered loudly, sending his voice down to Nate through the shadows. "Do you have any idea what time it is?"

Nate continued to stare up at him, and even though Brandon knew it had to be just his imagination playing tricks, he swore he could hear the sound of Nate's heart beating, steady, strong, above the song of the crickets.

"I know what time it is. It's time for me to talk to you. I don't think we've finished."

Head ruled over heart when Brandon replied, "Oh, I think we finished." But he didn't walk away, didn't disengage his gaze from Nate's.

"If that were true, you'd walk away. Listen, you need to hear what I have to say. Do me just that favor, and then the choice will be yours. I will leave or I will stay, but it will be up to you, and I promise to abide by any decision you make."

A car drifted by on Green Lake Way behind them. Brandon wondered what the driver was doing out in this lonely hour of the morning, and if he or she saw the two of them, looking as though they were enacting a modern-day, gay version of *Romeo and Juliet*.

"You want to come up?" Brandon asked.

"More than anything."

Brandon gripped the rail of the balcony, thinking. If he let Nate come up, he didn't know how much control he would have or if he could think clearly. Having him close, in his home, his private space, would definitely give the heart an advantage.

He was clearheaded enough to listen to his head, if only for the moment. A breeze moved across the surface of the lake, chilling him. Autumn was not far behind, the rush of wind reminded him.

"Give me a minute. I'll come down." Brandon turned before Nate had a chance to say anything more. Inside, he threw on a pair of cargo shorts, a T-shirt, and a pair of flip-flops. He grabbed his keys and headed out.

It felt almost surreal to be outside so early. It seemed the whole world was silent, sleeping, and that he and Nate were the only ones awake. It wasn't much of a stretch to imagine they were the only ones in the world.

He approached Nate, noting the sadness in his face. *Don't give me those puppy dog eyes. How can I believe anything coming from you? You're a master of fiction.*

"I'm glad you came out," Nate said, taking Brandon's hands and squeezing them between his own. "Thank you."

"What did you want to say?" Brandon gently disengaged his hands. "It's late. Or early. Whatever. I have to work tomorrow. Or today."

"Can we go somewhere?"

Brandon laughed. "Everything's closed."

"No, I mean, can we walk over by the lake again, maybe sit down?"

Brandon sighed. He didn't say anything, but he did let Nate take his hand and lead him. They crossed Green Lake Way and walked onto the grass bordering a playing field. "Here," Nate said, and the two of them sat in the dewy grass on a rise above the field.

In the distance, Brandon looked out at the shimmering blue-gray water, listening to the call of the first birds of morning, the quiet rush of the wind.

Nate put his arm around Brandon's shoulders and drew him close. Brandon had an impulse to shrug the arm and the caress away, feeling that Nate was not entitled any longer to touch him so intimately, but instead, he leaned into Nate's body, reveling in the simple pleasure of his warmth and the solidity of his presence.

"I don't have a lot to say, but I was thinking of something as I walked the circumference of the lake, trying to convince myself to go home." Nate began to speak, his words floating out into the darkness. He didn't look at Brandon, and Brandon pulled at the grass as Nate spoke.

But Brandon listened. He listened.

"I was thinking about love." Nate laughed softly. "I know that sounds like a line a romance writer would use, but it's true." He fell silent for a while. "I haven't told you much about my dad, other than the broad strokes. The truth is he was an alcoholic. Oh yeah, a high-functioning one—I never saw him drunk or anything like that—but every night, after work, he stopped at the American Legion and had four or five beers, then several more after he got home. He was usually asleep or passed out, I know now, by nine or ten every night."

Brandon wondered where this was heading but felt that to interrupt would be to break a spell.

"For many, many years, I resented the man. He was never an embarrassment. He held down his job, he took care of his family. But all that damn beer—well, it put up a wall between him and us. That wall never came down and stayed intact until the day he died.

"I resented him. Resented that he wasn't there for Hannah and me. For Mom. But then it came to me—I could only love the man he was, not the man I wanted him to be. I suspect that's a lesson many children have to learn. We grow up with these ideas of what parents should be, how they should revolve around us, what we think we deserve.

"It isn't until we're grown ourselves that we—if we're lucky—realize our parents are just people too, flawed."

He turned his head and met Brandon's eyes for a moment, then looked away. "What I thought about love tonight, Brandon, is that it's not about finding some model of perfection to love, but finding the person who's right for *you* and then embracing not only the good about them, but also the flaws. It's not just the good that makes them lovable, it's the stuff that gets in the way, the stuff we struggle to overcome to be better, that makes us human.

"And love—to me—is even more about embracing and accepting flaws than it is about celebrating the good we find."

Nate did meet Brandon's eyes now, full on. Brandon did not feel he was being sold a bill of goods, but instead realized that Nate was baring his soul to him. "Nate," he whispered softly, feeling he was drowning, but also feeling, just a tiny bit, that his head and heart were coming into synchronicity.

If he was drowning, the water was warm, welcoming.

Nate continued. "I'm a flawed person. I make mistakes. How I've handled my writing career might have been a mistake, and it might be one I have to pay dearly for. Who knows? And when I say pay, I am not talking about money.

"But the thing about people and their flaws is this: it's not that we have them, it's what we do with them.

"Brandon, whether we go anywhere from here or not is up to you, but even if we don't, I at least know I am a good person, and I know that I am doing the best I can to overcome my flaws. That's why I was at last honest with my readers and honest with you.

"I can only hope that you'll trust me enough to know that beneath my deception is a good person, an honest person, really." He gently stroked Brandon's cheek. "A person who loves you."

Brandon closed his eyes, allowing his mind to quiet, for dawn's breeze to wash over him. He realized that one of his own flaws might be being too rigid. Nate was right—love was about accepting not only the good about another person, but also their flaws.

It was also about something else, something Nate hadn't mentioned, but he would bet was in the other man's heart, because he was doing it right now.

Love was also about taking a leap into the unknown, making yourself vulnerable. It was a chance taken. It was a cosmic gamble. It was *faith*. It was a belief that happy endings could happen and did, every day. *That possibility could sustain us*, Brandon thought, *it has to*.

Otherwise, who, with the sense God gave them, would ever take such a risk, baring themselves to such heartache, if there wasn't also a promise of joy?

Maybe it wasn't so much a love of the flaws of another person that made love real, but the belief in the *possibility* of love, of having faith that things could work out.

Brandon knew, as he always had, he was helpless in the face of his heart, so he turned to Nate, placed his hand on the back of his neck, and drew him in for a long, lingering kiss. He hoped the kiss was eloquent, that it spoke of acceptance and forgiveness.

That it spoke of love.

When they at last pulled away, Brandon noticed a slight difference in the quality of light. Things were taking on more of a definition. The sky was brightening from gray to pale blue. More birds were singing. The sounds of cars behind them were coming more frequently.

He turned to Nate. "What you said earlier, that you would leave or you would stay?"

"Yeah?"

"I hope you'll stay." Brandon searched Nate's face for a sign of acceptance. What he saw instead was a quiet kind of joy. Nate didn't need to say a word.

This time, Brandon took Nate's hand as they stood, brushing grass cuttings and moisture from their butts, and led him toward his apartment building.

Toward *home.*

# Epilogue

The ferry from Anacortes glided through serene blue waters, gilded by the autumn sun. Islands and their rocky shorelines, all dotted with evergreens, rose up out of the water like the backs of beasts, passing by as the ferry sliced through the Salish Sea, skirting islands with names like Lopez, James, Blakely, all part of the body of islands known as San Juan. The wind off the water was cold, bracing, yet the sun, brilliant in a sky of blue dotted with only a few strands of cloud, like ribbons, was a warm contrast.

It was, in short, a lovely October day to sit out on the wide deck of the ferry and enjoy not only the breeze, but also the jaw-dropping scenery. The boat today was crowded with day-trippers, who were making their trip across the Strait of Juan de Fuca to the quaint maritime village of Friday Harbor. They would disperse and wander its village streets, stopping to shop, imbibe, and eat.

Eventually, the ferry would bring them back, but right now, none of them were thinking about that, only when the ferry would at last dock.

Brandon snuggled close to Nate, under an eave. The shadows cast by the eave made him cold, but Nate was like his own little furnace, giving off heat that was at once comforting and arousing.

He pressed his head against Nate's shoulder, remembering their morning together in Nate's bedroom.

They had awakened early, and even though the prior night had been filled with passion and about twenty different positions on multiple journeys toward ecstasy, they had come together, so to speak, once more as dawn invaded the room. That last time, Brandon recalled, had been the sweetest, with both of them still groggy from sleep, their bodies warm and languorous from the cocoon of sheets and pillows surrounding them. The most alive parts of their entire bodies were their cocks, which they pressed together as they kissed, morning mouths be damned. Even though there was no actual penetration, only a deep connection in their mouths and a friction that built steadily in intensity, threatening sparks, Brandon was left so satisfied after they both climaxed that he fell back asleep, oblivious to the glue of come sealing them together. When they awakened later in full morning, their stomachs and chests had looked as though there were patches of peeling skin on them.

Nate had gotten up while Brandon slept, gone downstairs and brought up a tray consisting of two mugs of coffee, croissants, scrambled eggs with cheese and green onion, and a plate of sliced oranges. There was also a gift bag on the tray, bright red.

"What's this?" Brandon had wondered, hefting the bag.

"A little something for you. Don't get excited. It's not an engagement ring." He had winked. "Not yet, anyway."

Brandon had peered into the bag and found that it contained a toothbrush, a couple pairs of Papi brand underwear, some socks (athletic footies and a few pairs of black cotton crew socks), an assortment of toiletries (razor, shaving gel, face scrub), and a loofah. He had looked up at Nate, grinning. "Thank you."

Nate had shrugged. "I thought it was time. You've been spending quite a few nights here, and I thought it would be easier than you dragging stuff to and from your place to mine. I cleared out a drawer in my bathroom for your bathroom stuff, and a drawer in here for your clothes." He had stroked Brandon's cheek, looking both tentative and happy. "I hope it's okay. I hope it's not too soon. I know you said you needed time to trust me."

Brandon had sat back against the headboard, not saying anything for a few minutes. He took a sip of his coffee, relishing the simple fact that Nate knew how he liked it: strong, with just a dollop of half-and-half and no sugar. He had been touched by the gesture, and he wondered if it was time to let go of his reservations about Nate. A couple of months had passed, and Nate had shown himself to be nothing more than an honest and giving man. He was not perfect by any means. He had that tendency to be online too much, blogging or chatting with fans on Facebook, or drifting away in the plot of his latest novel, a paranormal romance based on Irish Selkie legend with, of course, a gay Pacific Northwest twist. Sometimes Brandon had to pry him away from his keyboard.

But did he trust Nate?

Brandon did. He always had, really. But it was his head that stopped him from jumping in and moving too fast—making a rash move like moving in with Nate and his sister. But he had known, when he looked down on Nate that summer morning from his balcony and peered into his heart, that Nate was a good person, someone he could believe in. There are some things we know in our bones, instinctually, that we don't need our rational minds to tell us.

Hell, maybe he had known from the moment he first laid eyes on him at the Union bar.

And now, here they were, aboard a ferry and headed for a day of playing hooky. Even though Saturday was right next door, there was something liberating and special about making this day trip during a time when most of the world was at work.

"I'm so glad you could get the day off to do this." Nate shook his head. "I've lived in Seattle for a long time but have never had the opportunity to get up here to the San Juans. It's gorgeous." He turned to Brandon and kissed the tip of his nose. "*You're* gorgeous. What could be more perfect?"

Brandon smiled. "Oh, please! Save the schmaltz for your romance novels." He chuckled and ruffled Nate's hair. "It's just good to be here, and I thought Friday was the only day for Friday Harbor. I kind of like to think of it as appearing only on Fridays, like Brigadoon. Besides, there won't be as many tourists here today as there will be tomorrow and Sunday. I hate crowds."

"Well, we did bring a crowd of our own." Nate elbowed Brandon. "Look, there's two of them now."

And Brandon turned to watch Nate's sister and her new boyfriend, Walt, approach the rail overlooking the water. For Hannah, some good had come of the whole OpenHeartOpenMind fiasco, of duplicity and spying. Because he now knew Hannah had met what might be the love of *her* life that night in the Union bar, where Nate had originally gone to "let Brandon down gently."

That night must have been enchanted, because not one, but two, couples had emerged from it. Who said you could never meet anyone in a bar?

Brandon watched as Nate's redhead sister entwined her arm with Walt's, then leaned in close as the wind lifted her hair. Walt leaned down to plant a kiss on the top of her head and then moved away to point at something on the shoreline of Lopez Island.

"Think they'll stay together?" Nate wondered.

"Well, you should know better than I. You live with the woman."

Nate chuckled. "I have to remind myself of that lately. She's never there. She's all but moved in with him."

"But you like him?"

"He's all right, as straight guys go. No, really, he's a good guy. He even puts up with Marilyn." Nate grinned. "I like you better."

"Is that why I got a new toothbrush this morning?" Since they had, at the end of last summer, decided to make the leap into the chasm known as love with their hands clasped, they had also had the forethought to take things slow. They spent most weekends together and, although Brandon pined for Nate on the nights they were apart, he was glad they weren't rushing into anything. He never explicitly told Nate this, but he had simply let things play out, observing Nate to make sure his growing trust hadn't been misplaced. It was what the voice in his head, the one that sounded awfully like his mother, had told him to do.

Brandon could see the two of them, somewhere down the road, making their commitment to one another more official. Looking around at the stunning natural beauty surrounding them, he was glad for more than one reason that he and Nate lived in Washington State, where they could marry, if that happy day ever came to pass.

And in his heart, Brandon believed it would.

Who wouldn't want to live out their days with a romance writer? Brandon loved many things about Nate, but one of the things he loved most was his imagination, which he supposed was the thing that helped get their relationship off to its initial rocky start. Irony?

But he quickly came to see how handy an imagination could be, especially in the bedroom. Suddenly aroused, he leaned in and whispered, "How private are the men's rooms on this tub, anyway?"

Nate looked at him, a look of clearly feigned shock on his face. "Not very."

"Damn it. Maybe if you squat on the toilet seat so your feet don't show while I—"

Nate held up his hand. "Hold it right there. I am not about to get caught on a ferry on a fairy, if you know what I mean. They'll put us off at Lopez!"

"Ooh and look at those woods on that island. Think of what we could get up to! Boys in the sand!"

"Down, boy. Let's have a nice day with our friends and family. Then we go home to my place for more of the naughty stuff. I may not let you out of bed *all* weekend." Nate paused. "Hannah's staying at Walt's."

Brandon sighed, giving a surreptitious swipe at his crotch, which was bulging. "You're just making things worse."

They sat in silence for a while, listening to the shrill cry of a gull as it soared through the sky, the low drum of the ferry engine, laughter from the deck above.

After a while, Brandon wondered, "Is Marilyn taking things any better?"

When Hannah and Walt's attraction had started to look like it was developing into something more lasting and significant, Hannah's BFF had gotten very jealous, to the point where Brandon and Nate had wondered if the woman belonged to the same church as they, so to speak. There had been some rough times for the two friends, but then Marilyn had gone out one night about a month ago with Brandon and Nate to the R Place. Marilyn had asked if she could tag along because, as she put it, she had been "spurned" by her starry-eyed pal. "Her highness no longer has time for me," she had lamented, rolling her eyes.

That night, Marilyn had met Brandon's horndog friend, Christian, and the two, as unlikely a pair as one could imagine, had become fast friends. It wasn't so unlikely, though, as Nate had to remind Brandon when he puzzled over it, if you thought about all they had in common—both were crazy for cock and cocktails. They had quickly bonded, rating asses and baskets as they came into the bar.

Now Marilyn was a fixture at places like the dark, leathery Cuff and, as they all knew, took a kind of perverse pleasure in seeing her new best pal, Christian, hook up.

Sometimes Brandon wondered if she *literally* saw him hook up now and again, but he didn't want to examine that suspicion too closely.

Besides, he had his own man now.

They were preparing to dock, and there was a rustle of activity on the boat as the passengers headed for the bow to disembark.

"I wish we could just stay here." Brandon snuggled closer to Nate. "No telling what we could find to occupy us." He waggled his eyebrows. "A whole boat to ourselves? All those levels? Just waiting for our special way of christening."

"Oh, I have some ideas. But later, later." Nate stood and held out a hand. "C'mon, let's go meet up with the rest of the gang. I want to be sure Marilyn and Christian are stable enough to walk off the boat." He winked at Brandon. "I saw the flask of vodka she had in that oversized bag she lugs around. Those two had Mimosas for days, okay?"

Brandon stood. "They'll probably head for the nearest bar."

"And we'll head for the nearest bushes, sweetheart."

"Don't say things you don't mean," Brandon admonished.

"I gave that up a while back." Nate looked into his eyes, and even now, after a few months of being together, Brandon was still electrified by that simple liquid connection. "I am all about what you see is what you get these days—thanks to you."

Brandon felt a surge of love course through him, and, in spite of the passengers hurrying around them as the big boat drifted toward the dock, he pulled Nate to him and kissed him, eyes wide open.

What he saw was what he got, yes, but it was also what he had always wanted.

# About the Author

Real Men. True Love.

Rick R. Reed is an award-winning and bestselling author of more than fifty works of published fiction. He is a Lambda Literary Award finalist. Entertainment Weekly has described his work as "heartrending and sensitive." Lambda Literary has called him: "A writer that doesn't disappoint..." Find him at rickrreedreality.blogspot.com. Rick lives in Palm Springs, CA, with his husband, Bruce, and their fierce Chihuahua/Shiba Inu mix, Kodi.

Email: rickrreedbooks@gmail.com

Facebook: www.facebook.com/rickrreedbooks

Twitter: @rickrreed

# Other NineStar books by this author

*Unraveling*
*Sky Full of Mysteries*
*The Perils of Intimacy*
*IM*
*Chaser*
*Raining Men*
*Blue Umbrella Sky*
*Third Eye*
*Legally Wed*

# Coming Soon from Rick R. reed

## Big Love

### PROLOGUE

Dane Bernard, a big, gentle man, a teacher, would always look at that particular first day of school at Summitville High School as the one that changed his life forever.

Three things happened in that one momentous day that made returning to his old, comfortable life impossible—he rescued a boy from bullies, he lost his wife of twenty years, and...he began a journey to find himself.

How these three events, seemingly so disparate, tie together is our story. Let's begin with the first.

### CHAPTER ONE

Truman Reid was white as a stick of chalk—skin so pale it was nearly translucent. His blue eyes were fashioned from icy spring water. His hair—platinum blond—lay in curls across his forehead and spilled down his neck. He was the kind of boy for whom adjectives like "lovely" and "pretty" would most definitely apply. More than once in his life, he was mistaken for a girl.

When he was a very little boy, well-meaning strangers (and some not so well-meaning) would ask if he was a boy or a girl. Truman was never offended by the question, because he could see no shame in being mistaken for a girl. It wasn't until later that he realized there were some who would think the question offensive.

But this boy, who, on the first day of school, boldly and some might say unwisely wore a T-shirt that proclaimed "It Gets Better" beneath an image of a rainbow flag, didn't seem to possess the pride the T-shirt proclaimed. At Summitville High School, even though it was 2015, one did not shout out one's sexual orientation, not in word, not in fashion, and certainly not in deed.

Who knew what caused Truman to break with convention that morning when he made up his mind to wear that T-shirt on the first day of school? It wasn't like he needed to proclaim anything—after all, the slight, effeminate boy had been the object of bullies and torturers since, oh, about second grade. Truman could never "pass."

He was a big sissy. It was a fact and one Truman had no choice but to accept.

His shoulders, perpetually hunched, hunched farther during his grade school and junior high years, when such epithets as "sissy," "fag," "pansy," and "queer" were hurled at him in school corridors and playgrounds on a daily basis. Truman knew the old schoolyard chant wasn't true at all—words could and did hurt. And so, occasionally, did fists and hands.

And yet, despite the teasing—or maybe it's more apt to say because of it—Truman was not ashamed of who and what he was. His single mom, Patsy, his most vocal supporter and defender, often told him the same thing.

"God made you just the way you are, honey. Beautiful. And if you're one of his creations, there's nothing wrong in who you are. You just hold your head up and be proud." The sad truth was, Patsy would often tell her boy stuff like this as she brushed tears away from his face.

It wasn't only tears she brushed away, though. Her unconditional love also brushed away any doubt Truman might have had that he was anything other than a normal boy, even though he was not like most of the boys his age in Summitville, Ohio, that backward little burg situated on the Ohio River and in the foothills of the Appalachian Mountains. In spite of the teasing and the bullying—and the pain they caused—Truman wasn't ashamed of who he was, which was what led him to wearing the fated T-shirt that got him in so much trouble his first day as a freshman at Summitville High School.

The incident occurred near the end of the day, when everyone was filing into the school gymnasium for an orientation assembly and a speech from the school's principal, Doug Calhoun, on what the returning students and incoming freshmen could expect that year.

Truman was in the crush of kids making their way toward the bleachers. High school was no different than grade school or junior high in that Truman was alone. And even though this was the first day of school, Truman already had a large three-ring binder tucked under his arm, along with English Composition, Biology, and Algebra I textbooks. Tucked into the notebook and books were papers—class schedules of assignments and the copious notes the studious Truman had already taken.

Kirk Samson, a senior and starting quarterback on the football team, knew the laughs he could get if he tripped this little fag in his pride-parade T-shirt, so he held back a little in the crowd, waiting for just the right moment to thrust out a leg in front of the unsuspecting Truman, whose eyes were cast down to the polished gymnasium floor.

Truman didn't see the quarterback's leg until it was too late, and he stumbled, going down hard on one knee. That sight was not the funniest thing the crowd had seen, although the pratfall garnered a roar of appreciative laughter at Truman's expense. But what was funnier was when Truman's notebook, books, and papers all flew out from under his arm, landing in a mess on the floor.

Kirk, watching from nearby with a smirk on his face, whispered two words to the kids passing by: "Kick 'em. Kick 'em."

And the kids complied, sending Truman's notes, schedules, and texts across the gym floor, as Truman, on his knees, struggled to gather everything up, even as more and more students got in on the fun of sending them farther and farther out of his reach.

Now, that was the funniest thing the crowd had seen.

Who knows how long the hilarity would have gone on if an authority figure had not intervened?

*

Dane Bernard, English teacher, gentle giant, cross-country track coach, and indisputably one of the most well-liked teachers at the school, saw what was happening to Truman and rushed over. He only wished he could have been quicker to act—the boy's books and papers were now kicked out almost to the middle of the gym floor.

Dane knelt down by Truman, though, and helped him pick everything up as the kids behind, their laughter dying to a few isolated giggles, scrambled for their seats among the bleachers. It took a long time for the titters and whispering to die down.

Once the papers had been haphazardly gathered and even more haphazardly stuffed back inside notebook and textbooks, Dane put what he hoped was a calming hand on Truman's shoulder and gave it a little squeeze.

"You okay, son?" he asked.

The boy didn't have to respond. Dane frowned as he took in the tears standing in the boy's eyes. "What's your name?"

"Truman. Truman Reid." As befitting his name, the slight boy's voice came out reedy, a little high, still cracking, the bane of adolescent males since time immemorial.

"I'm Mr. Bernard."

Truman stared up at Dane, and as he did, a tear dribbled down his cheek, across a couple of acne bumps, to land on the floor. "Thanks. Thanks for helping me." Truman wiped away any remaining tears with the back of his hand. "I should get to my seat."

Dane looked over at the crowd, many of whom were watching, giggles ready to burst forth from their mean little faces. Dane thought there was no creature crueler on God's green earth than the teenage boy or girl. He squeezed Truman's shoulder. "Listen, the assembly's no biggie. Rules and regulations. Making sure you have 'an attitude that will determine your altitude.' Crap like that. You wanna skip it?" With a gentle smile, Dane tried to convey he cared. "We could go sit together someplace quiet for a bit and just chat." Dane shrugged. "No pressure."

"I don't know." The boy looked toward the crowd. Dane was disheartened when he followed his gaze. He didn't see one welcoming face.

"Come on," Dane said. "I've got Starburst in my homeroom."

"Well then, if you've got Starburst, how can I possibly say no?" And at last Truman smiled.

That smile was the kind of thing that made Dane get up every morning and come to work.

"Follow me."

Dane led the boy along the school corridor—green tile floors bracketed on either side by rows and rows of lockers in the same shade of industrial green. The boy, Truman, stopped at one of the lockers and began trying to work its combination lock. Dane paused to watch, figuring the boy wanted to divest himself of the load of books and papers he lugged around. Who had so much stuff on the first day of the semester?

Truman whispered what sounded like a curse to Dane as he did battle with the lock. He couldn't get it. He tried several times, spinning and spinning to no good effect. His books and papers once more tumbled to the floor. The situation was so sad, so pathetic, it almost made Dane want to laugh. Not at the boy, no, but at the absurdity of life and how it could simply be so plain cruel as to kick this harmless-looking boy when he was so down.

Dane didn't laugh. He neared Truman as the boy crumpled to the floor, sobbing.

Dane squatted next to him and patted his back. "It's okay. It's okay. Get your things together. We can get your combination from the janitor. No prob. Come on. Pick your stuff up and come back to my office."

Dane's heart just about broke as the boy looked up at him, cheeks damp and snot on his upper lip. What a way to start the year! He took in the shirt the boy was wearing and thought he might as well have affixed one of those

"Kick Me" signs to his back before starting school this morning. Why ask for trouble? Dane wondered. Maybe he could figure the kid out once he got him to his office. Maybe he could let him know that some things that were personal should remain that way.

Truman stood, unsteady, a colt getting to its feet for the first time. He looked wildly around, like he was trapped there in the corridor. "I wanna go home," Truman said, voice barely above a whisper.

"Don't you wanna talk?" Dane asked, his eyebrows coming together with concern. "You'll find my homeroom is a judgment-free zone."

"I want to go home," Truman repeated, his voice a little louder.

"Do you walk to school?"

Truman shook his head.

"Buses won't be here for—" Dane glanced down at his watch, a Fossil timepiece with an orange band his wife, Katy, had gotten him last Christmas. "—another forty-five minutes. Come on. We'll wait in my homeroom." To repeat the offer of Starburst seemed like a silly incentive now. "Let's just go there and chill a little. You're a freshman, right?"

Truman nodded.

Dane grinned. "Come on. How many chances will you get to skip out on an assembly with a teacher? You like books?"

Truman nodded.

"Good. I teach English. You'd be surprised how many kids don't, how the only things they read are text messages, tweets, and status updates on Facebook. Who do you like to read?" Dane started walking toward his homeroom, hoping to coax Truman along.

"I like Stephen King and Dean Koontz," Truman said, not moving. "And I wanna go home."

"I like them too. I read my first King when I was about your age. Christine, I think it was. You read that one? About the possessed car? Sick!"

"Look, sir, you're being really nice and all, but I need to get home. I know the final bell hasn't rung yet, but do you think you could let me slide? I don't have to tell you I've had a rotten day, and I just need to get home, where I can hide."

Dane shook his head, not to refuse Truman's request but at the sadness of how the boy viewed home. "Where do you live?"

"Little England. It's only a mile or so from here."

Dane scratched his chin. Little England was one of the poorest neighborhoods in Summitville, bordered by the Ohio River on one side and railroad tracks on the other. The neighborhood, sitting just below river level, was regularly flooded. The houses there were mostly adorned with rusting aluminum siding. Or they were wooden frame in need of paint. Little England was poor. Dirty. And for Truman, Dane supposed, it was home.

"I can walk. Can you just look the other way? Please? Just for today?" Tears sprung up in Truman's eyes again. "I could use a break."

Dane so wanted to say yes, but there would be consequences if something should happen to the boy on his way home. Serious consequences, the kind where he could lose his job. And with twenty years here at the school, two kids and a wife to support, he couldn't let that happen. Yet the terror and pain on this boy's face rent his heart in two. "Tell you what," Dane said finally. "If you can call someone to come get you—your mom or your dad—I can let you go with them. Otherwise—" Dane stopped himself as he watched Truman pull a phone out of his pocket. His fingers flew over the tiny screen. Dane was amazed how even the poorest of kids these days managed to have cell phones.

Truman didn't look at him. Instead he stared at the screen as if willing it to life. After a minute or so, Truman breathed a sigh of relief. He held the screen of the flip phone up so Dane could see. Dane read the shorthand texts, which basically confirmed that Mom could get off from work and pick him up in ten minutes, but she wanted to know what was wrong.

What wasn't wrong? Dane imagined Truman thinking.

"Can I go wait outside?" Truman asked.

Dane sighed. "Sure you don't want to come talk to me? Just for a few minutes? We'll see your mom pull up from my window."

"You just have to make this as hard as you can, don't you?" Truman snapped.

Dane's smile faltered. "I was trying to do just the opposite," he said.

Truman's face reddened. "I'm sorry, man. I just need to get home."

Dane nodded. "I get it. Go ahead. Wait outside for your mom."

Truman started away, walking quickly, books still stuffed under one matchstick arm.

Dane called after him, "Come talk to me tomorrow. We'll get your locker combination figured out." Among other things, Dane thought as he turned to head back to his homeroom.

Once there, Dane plopped down in his imitation-leather desk chair and sighed. He rubbed his hands over his face. Seeing kids teased and bullied was, unfortunately, part of the job, and over two decades, Dane had lost count of the number of times he had witnessed cruelty. Sometimes he thought high school students had cornered the market on unkindness.

But Truman Reid bothered him more than most. It was that damn T-shirt he wore, one that might as well have proclaimed "I'm a big old fag" on the front, instead of its message of hope and the pride of the rainbow flag. Kids here just looked for any excuse to tease, to belittle. The jocks especially seemed to feel that someone's being gay was as good a reason as any to make their life a living hell.

Dane was just about to reflect on the relevance being gay had on his own life when his phone rang. For a moment he was grateful for the ringtone, because it saved him from some of his darkest ruminations, thoughts he shared with no one, but which Truman—with his damnable and enviable pride—had brought out in him.

He pulled his iPhone from his pocket and glanced down at the screen. Unknown, Caller ID taunted him. Dane was tempted not to answer, to just let it go to voice mail and head for the student assembly so he could at least say he'd been there, but instead he pressed Accept.

"Dane Bernard here." He fully expected a telemarketer.

"Mr. Bernard." A male voice came over the line. "Is this the husband of Katherine Bernard?"

A chill coursed through him. "Yup." He tried to swallow, but the sudden dryness in his mouth nearly prevented it. "Is everything all right?"

"I'm sorry to tell you this, Mr. Bernard, but there's been an accident involving your wife. This is Bill Rogers, by the way, with the State Highway Patrol."

Dane could feel his whole body go cold, as if dipped in ice water. "But she's okay, right?" he managed to gasp.

The man responded, "Do you think you could come down to City Hospital? I'll meet you at the ER. Just ask for Bill Rogers. I'll wait."

"Is she okay?" Dane repeated, gripping the phone—hard. But the patrolman had already hung up.

# Also Available from NineStar Press

# Connect with NineStar Press

www.ninestarpress.com

www.facebook.com/ninestarpress

www.facebook.com/groups/NineStarNiche

www.twitter.com/ninestarpress

www.tumblr.com/blog/ninestarpress

www.ingramcontent.com/pod-product-compliance
Lightning Source LLC
Chambersburg PA
CBHW061607100726
47898CB00002B/568